1.99

18/12

Henshaw

Two

Short Story

Competition Prize Winners

2015-2017

Editor: Graham Jennings

Editorial Office: Henshawpress, 24 Rowlandson Close,
Northampton, NN3 3PB

Tel: 01604 407934

Email: henshawpress@outlook.co.uk

Web site: www.henshawpress.co.uk

ISBN – 13: 978-1540766533

ISBN-10: 1540766535

Foreword

This anthology is the second to be produced by Henshawpress and contains thirty three of the prize winning and highly commended stories from our Henshaw Short Story Competitions over the past two years.

It is an eclectic mix of lovely stories of human relations: romance, crime, humour, ghosts, science fiction, and politics all are here. There is something for everyone. It is full of previously unpublished stories that are both thought and emotion provoking and will bring tears to your eyes and smiles to your lips.

I would like to give thanks to these and all the other authors who have entered our competitions, to the Judges, who give their time voluntarily. To all those who have given support to Henshawpress, in particular to David Jennings, Jim Latham, Kate McGrail and Susan McKernon many thanks.

Graham Jennings

CONTENTS

LOST IN THOUGHT
by
Nathaniel Mellor

James stared out the car window, drawing shapes on the condensation collecting inside.

"Doin' okay there, sport?" His father, in the driver's seat next to him, asked. He liked to call James "sport" or "pal." Even "kiddo." It didn't matter that James was twenty-seven and had lived alone for the better part of ten years.

"Yeah, Dad. Doing okay." James said, somewhere between sarcasm and honesty. Even he couldn't decide how he felt.

"Wanna talk about it?" His dad offered.

James focused on the fish he was drawing, adding squiggles for water and sharp angles for scales.

"Yeah. No. Not now, at least."

His father nodded, understanding. Flicking the directional downwards, James's father made a right turn. A horn blared from behind their car.

"Where are we going?" James looked up from his window masterpiece.

"Remember when you and I would go out for the afternoon and run by Checkers on the way home?

And your mom never found out because I wouldn't let us leave until you finished everything? Hah! She would have been pissed to see a milkshake cup in the trash." His father smiled a half-smile.

"And you want to go again *now*?" James questioned him.

"Yes." His father answered, pulling into an empty parking lot.

James opened his door and stood up, stretching. Looking at the sky, he squinted. It always seemed to rain on the day funerals were held. Never a tree-snapping thunderstorm, but a dreary pitter-patter of rain.

They walked up to the order window and stood in the bright white light of the food display board.

"Number seven with a vanilla milkshake?" James's father asked, smiling slightly as if it were an old joke.

"C'mon Dad, you know I'm vegan now."

"Your choice." His dad turned to the order window and waited patiently for a server to come. He didn't wait long.

"Welcome to Checkers, what do you want?" The lady asked, after opening the window.

"One number seven with a chocolate milkshake." James's father ordered.

"One number seven with a chocolate milkshake. Will that be all?" The lady asked.

James's father looked to James, and James waved away his chance to order.

"That'll be all, then." James's father handed over his card. After a few beats, she handed it back with a receipt.

"Your food will be out shortly." She said, and closed the window.

James and his father stood in silence under the awning, watching as cars did their stop-and-go dance through the drive-thru.

Finally, the window opened and a young man with acne pushed the food towards them, and closed the window again without a word.

"Should we sit out here?" James's father asked.

"Dad, it's raining." James said.

"They have umbrellas." His father responded.

"And this is a Ralph Lauren jacket." James held his lapels.

His father shrugged and stood there with his white food bag getting increasingly more transparent.

James shook his head and walked back to the car with his father in tow.

Once they were situated comfortably, James's father opened his paper bag and reached down, pulling out a fry.

"Are you going to eat here? In the parking lot?" James questioned him, despite the fact he was obviously eating in the parking lot.

"We don't get to talk anymore, kiddo. I think we should talk." His father replied, ignoring James's question.

"Fine. What do you want to talk about?" James snapped.

"Am I wrong in thinking we used to be friends?" James's father asked,

James paused, then responded. "No, Dad. We used to be close."

"Then what happened to us? Because for the life of me, I can't figure out what it was." James's father asked, putting the bag of food on the dashboard.

"Can I ask you a question?" James countered.

"Sure, pal."

"When did you stop loving my mom?"

James's father looked at James in something bordering on shock and curiosity. "What makes you say I stopped loving her?"

"Dad?" James asked.

"Yeah?"

"Can you not treat me like a child? Believe it or not, I did grow up somewhere between turning fifteen and turning twenty-five."

"Fair enough, James. You want this to be a man-to-man talk?"

"No. I want it to be a father-to-son talk."

James's father turned away, nodding a few times. "I have never stopped loving your mother. However, you're right in a way. We were no longer in love with each other."

"How?" James asked. "People don't just fall out of love."

"Don't they? People fall in love pretty easily. Sometimes it only takes a few minutes or the cost of a drink. Sometimes it's a more drawn out affair. But in the end, falling in love usually happens quickly."

"So you just fell out of love with Mom?"

James's father rubbed his eyes with the heels of his hands. "We were moving in different directions. It sounds like such a joke, doesn't it?" James's father smiled at James but James didn't return the gesture. There were tears in James's eyes.

"It happened four years ago."

"Why didn't you tell me?" James asked.

"You were stressed enough." James's father answered simply.

"And you guys didn't get a divorce? Go your separate ways, or whatever?"

"We couldn't. We just found out she was sick."

"And now she's dead. Is that why you didn't cry at the funeral? Because you're finally free?"

"Is that what you think?" James's father snapped. "You think I'm happy that I just buried your mother?"

"Well you don't seem too beaten up at the fact." James tried to lash out but he started to realize he just took a step in the wrong direction. He let his anger dictate his words.

"How old are you, James? Twenty-seven?" His father asked, all traces of friendship gone. "What do you know of the world? Do you know the last time I heard from you before I called you a week ago telling you your mother died? A year ago. You called me to ask for money, money that your mother needed."

"Then why even give it to me?" James interrupted. "If Mom needed it so badly, why would you lend me the money?"

"Your mother wanted me to. She believed in what you were doing, even if I didn't."

"And now you blame me for it?"

"Jesus Christ! Do you ever listen? I have never once blamed you for asking for money. And after everything your mother did for you, you didn't even visit. Not once that I can remember."

"I know you don't, Dad." James sounded defeated.

"So where were you when she would spit and swear because she knew her sentences didn't make sense? Where were you to help her bathe, and to dress her?" James's father spit out every word. "And where were you when she forgot who you were? Or where and when she was?" He whispered. "Where were you?"

"I'm sorry, Dad." James said.

"Me too, James. Me too. You know, she was looking for you at the end. She asked for her little Jamison. I didn't have the heart to tell her the truth. She thought you were in the kitchen. Or the living room. That you just stepped out. At the end, I think she knew. I think she knew you were gone."

"I get it! You don't think I'm a good son. You have made that perfectly clear, so clear in fact, that you were ready to step out of our lives if Mom hadn't gotten sick."

"When did you get so self-centred and ignorant?" James's father erupted.

"Is that what you think I am?" James asked. "An egotistical prick that cares only about himself?"

"You haven't shown me you aren't. Maybe it's because you're young, or maybe you've lived away for too long, but you've become a poor excuse for a son. I hope that by the time you're my age, you'll have some more respect for those who have given you everything they didn't have." James's father opened the car door and walked to the trashcan, without bothering to hunch over to protect himself from the rain. With a contemptuous toss, he threw away his number seven (minus one fry) and chocolate milkshake.

James sat in the car, wiping away the fish and water. They would go back to their home in Mastic Beach, and James would go upstairs to bed. And when he woke up, his father would be at the kitchen table crying over his youngest son who didn't live there anymore. And James would tell him, "I live upstairs Dad. I moved back in two years ago to take care of you and mom."

And when the day after tomorrow came, he would repeat it all over again.

CROSSROADS

by

Barbara Young

She's at the till, she's panicking. The queue behind her fidgets. Half her groceries are packed and she can't find her purse. I wait. I'm close to her, counting slowly to ten, enjoying the tension. Everyone wants to be involved, making suggestions and sympathy noises. The checkout girl, the queue, they're all watching. Then, I lean in and save the day.

"I think this is yours. You dropped it by the wines." I hold out a very nice soft leather purse, which bulges with cash and credit cards. It had been quite a temptation, but I resisted.

A slim hand, immaculately manicured, extends towards the purse and grasps it greedily.

"Oh, thank you so much. It must have fallen out of my bag when I tripped up."

Yes, I had seen my moment when you were distracted and I lifted the object in question from your bag. A neat manoeuvre, in and out, and no-one the wiser. Pete would be proud. He taught me everything I know.

I smile and shrug an "it's nothing" gesture at her business suit and her precision cut hair. Her glance takes in my clothes and my hair, seems to find me wanting, and she turns back to the girl on the till. A few beeps, the flash of a credit card and she is on her way. I watch her climb into a small red sports car and drive out of the car park. That's okay. I know where she lives.

Tara drops her bags of grocery onto the kitchen table and kicks off her shoes. It has been a bitch of a day. One of her clients had made a complaint about her and her boss had given her a patronising diatribe on how to curry favour with scumbags. Since when did being a successful criminal give one carte blanche to make a grab for your solicitor's ass? She has had enough of working for these idiots, kowtowing to the blatantly guilty and manipulating the law to ensure justice is rarely done. It's time for a change.

Then, there was that awful moment in the supermarket when she thought she had lost her purse. How the hell had she managed to drop it? And the tall, scruffy girl who had found it; well that just goes to show that wearing a hoody doesn't necessarily make you a bad person. The girl could have just kept the cash. A stab of guilt: she hadn't really thanked her properly; she'd been panicking at the time.

Tara sighs and pulls a bottle of wine from one of the grocery bags. Snagging a glass from the drainer she twists the top off the bottle and fills the glass almost to the top. Sod letting it breathe, she tips it to her lips and gulps greedily. When she sets the glass down, it is half empty.

She pulls out a chair, sits down and props her feet up on the table. Her gaze flicks around the shiny top-of-the-range kitchen. There's not much comfort to be found in a pristine ceramic hob or a complicated coffee machine. Gadgets are no substitute for warm living bodies. She shakes her head; not going there again. More wine is needed.

She jumps slightly as the doorbell sounds.

I push the bell and hear muffled chimes, some naff classical tune. I am chewing my lip. I will not be intimidated by the size of the house, by the lush garden or the crunchy gravel drive. She's even got a kidney shaped fish pond and I'm not going to spit in it. The door opens and there she is, wine glass in hand.

"Hello. Can I help you?" she asks.

She doesn't even recognise me. People like her never notice people like me. I dig into the back pocket of my jeans and pull out a credit card.

"I think this must be yours. I found—"

She cuts me off. "Oh, it's you. The girl in the supermarket." She takes the credit card, frowns at it. "Yes it's mine. I'd forgotten I had that one."

How many credit cards has she got? I don't even have one. I'm a cash only kind of girl.

"I found it on the floor, by the wines after you'd left," I say. She swallows the lie and I'm chewing my lip again, looking past her into the glossy hallway, avoiding eye contact.

She's glassy-eyed and the wine in her hand is sloshing around. I really hadn't expected her to be a plonky; this weighs in my favour. She hasn't questioned how I know her address.

"You'd better come in. I didn't thank you properly." She turns and gestures vaguely at the inside of the house. I didn't think it would be this easy. I follow her into a massive kitchen. It is clean and shiny. Stainless steel shimmers. We sit at a dark wooden table and she waves a bottle at me.

"Do you want a drink?" she asks.

Normally, I'm strictly a can of lager kind of girl but this is anything but normal. I nod my assent.

Tara pours the girl a glass of red and studies her across the table. There is something familiar about the set of her eyes and the slightly squared off jawline.

She tilts her head and squints a little. "Do I know you?" she asks.

The girl gives a hard little laugh. "I doubt it. I'm Gemma and I don't knock around this type of place as a rule."

Tara takes in the long brown hair piled up in a tight knot on the girl's head, the nose ring, the worn jeans and ubiquitous hoody. She is clean, but somehow worn down, looks about seventeen but is probably older. Tara has represented kids like this in court. Never an optimistic outcome.

"Most people wouldn't have handed in that purse, or not before taking the cash first." Tara doesn't voice the shameful "people like you" she is thinking. She wonders if the girl can hear her thoughts.

"I need to thank you properly." Tara, aware she's repeating herself, pulls a twenty pound note from the purse and waves it at Gemma. "Please, take it."

Gemma ignores the note. She tips her glass to her lips, grimaces and downs the contents in one. Tara watches as the girl helps herself to another one and stands up, wandering around the kitchen, fingers trailing slowly along granite worktops. Opening and closing doors, occasionally glancing sideways at Tara, then pacing on.

"Nice place you've got here," says Gemma. "It's big for just one person."

Tara is beginning to feel rattled. How does the girl know she lives alone? She could be an ex client, but even so she wouldn't know details of her private life. Tara is always careful not to reveal any personal facts to the people she represents. Very unfair when you think about it; they have to reveal so much of their lives to their solicitor.

"Well, it suits me, and I like the area. There's a big park at the bottom of the street, great for walking. It's always full of kids and dogs, lads playing football, throwing Frisbees." Tara doesn't add that she never goes to the park. That the kids' laughter strums at her nerves and the barking, muddy dogs that leap up make her want to scream at their smug owners.

"And it's quiet; the neighbours keep themselves to themselves." Tara knows she is babbling, but there is something about this whole scene that feels off. She is sitting in her own house, in her own kitchen, at her own table. So why does she feel like the stranger?

I'm having fun. I really didn't expect that. Actually Tara's alright. Generous with the old vino and oh so grateful for my little act of mercy. I can see she doesn't quite know what to do with me now. Probably regrets inviting me in but is too polite to ask me to leave. I'll keep her on the back foot a little longer.

"Must be well paid, the solicitor thing." I gesture at all the shiny bright appliances and out of the window at the rolling green lawn."

Tara gives a little frown and shakes her head. I can see I'm pushing it now and she's getting suspicious.

"I didn't tell you I was a solicitor," says Tara, with a confused look on her face. "Did I?"

"A place like this; must be alarmed, cameras, the works." I know fine well it's alarmed, I saw the keypad by the front door as I came in. Basic model not linked to the police or the security company; just loud ringing bells supposed to frighten off the big bad burglars.

"What do you want? How do you know I'm a solicitor?" Tara puts down her glass. She's wobbling a bit. I must have drunk as much as her, but I'm used to stronger stuff than alcohol. "Have I represented you?"

So, there it is. The only way she can think of that our paths might have crossed is via the courts. How little she knows. I could let her off the hook and tell her, but it has taken me so long to track her down, to check all the facts, that I'm not sure I want to. My plan doesn't extend much beyond the front door.

"You think, because I look like this." I gesture to my charity shop clothes. "And you look like that." I wave at her smart business suit, though it's looking a bit rumpled now. "That we must have met in court." My voice is rising, I'm angry. I take a breath, calm myself. But, I can see her thinking: traumatic childhood, the care system, abuse, drugs, the courts. She's wrong about most of it. My foster parents were okay, but they were in it for the money, not the kids. Looks like Tara got the better deal. The problem was me, my anger—it still is.

"I'm sorry, Gemma, I really didn't mean to upset you." Tara puts a hand on my arm leads me to the table, sits me down. "Let me make you a coffee before you go. We've both had a lot of wine and I could do with some caffeine."

Credit where it's due, she seemed a bit scared of me a minute ago, now she is simply concerned. As she puts the cup of coffee down, I notice her perfect nails are false, one of them has broken off and the real nail is bitten to a bloody quick. What I have seen of this perfect house seems cold and dead; it makes my crummy flat seem almost cosy.

I slurp the scalding coffee down in two goes and stand up. "I'd better be on my way. I'm glad you got your purse back and thanks for the wine."

"Thanks for the company. Friday night, I should be out partying." Tara gives me a tight smile and looks me straight in the eye. "I know we've met somewhere before," she says.

I'm out the door like a shot, down the drive and at the bus stop. I didn't really have a clear plan when I came here tonight. I knew my older sister was living in a posh area and doing okay as a solicitor. She had never bothered to look for me, since we were split up as kids and sent in different directions, so why should I care? I thought I would talk my way in and maybe nick some stuff. Laugh about it with Pete afterwards.

Now, I see she is as broken as I am. Well, maybe just seriously chipped around the edges, but she certainly isn't the confident, successful woman I expected. This cheers me; shallow I know. Maybe, just maybe, I will return and tell her who I am. Find out what happened.

TRAVELLER'S REST
by
Lucy Brighton

"You see, I told you I would take you to Mablethorpe in my car eventually didn't I?" Closing the door behind her, I climbed into the driver's seat and adjusted the mirrors; it had become second nature. I took a final breath and turned the ignition. This was going to be a difficult journey.

I eased out of the drive with the expertise of a pro even though I had only been driving a few short weeks. My mum usually joked that I could have shares in the DVLA by now, but today she said nothing. Despite the bright blue sky, the temperature in the car was cold; I turned up the heat and waited for the old fan to churn into action. The car had been a bargain. It had been one of the happiest days of my life when I handed over the £400 in an array of notes and received the keys. Despite being my hardest earned possession, it didn't afford many luxuries such as heating or electric windows. In fact, one of the windows didn't open at all. It didn't matter. I smiled in her direction.

"We are on our way."

I looked over at her, "Shall we put the radio on? It's going to be a long drive?" She didn't mind the hours of tedium; Mablethorpe was her favourite place in the world. We had spent every year holidaying in the small seaside town for as long as I could remember and every year the journey had been traumatic to say the least. It started with a dilapidated train to Sheffield, followed by a connecting train to Skegness and finally a long, claustrophobic bus journey to Mablethorpe. I think I started learning to drive just so I wouldn't have to endure that trip every June. If she could keep positive about that long haul, then I knew a few hours in the relative comfort of the car wouldn't phase her.

Once we were on the motorway, the scenery changed from the picturesque views of our little village to the dull grey tarmac which stretched out endlessly in front of us. The motorway would take us almost all of the way there. I swallowed hard at the thought of arriving, at seeing the sea with its myriad of colours, sea life and undercurrents. A slide show of memories at that beach played in my mind. I could see myself a child again jumping over the waves and squealing with excitement. The old tin bucket abandoned next to a carefully constructed sand castle, a flag protruding proudly from the top. I could almost taste the salt water and the ever present crunch of sand.

Ring Ring. Wrenched from my memories, I blinked several times and focused on the phone in the holder affixed to the window. 'Jake' was blazoned on the screen. I could feel her eyes looking disapprovingly at me. Keeping my eyes focused on the road, I tried to pretend it wasn't ringing as a scarlet rash spread from my chest to my cheeks. My knuckles whitened and I pressed a little firmer on the accelerator.

I knew I was an idiot for going back out with him and I didn't need her telling me that. I didn't need a lecture or it spelling out to me. I was a grown woman, I told myself. That's why I had kept it a secret, not because I wanted to deceive her. Well there were no more secrets now. "Look mum," I began, "It's complicated, ok. What happened with him and that Karen was a mistake. And you know it was really more her than him. I mean she practically stalked him." I knew I was sounding more and more ridiculous with every passing second. My voice had risen to a shrill pitch, almost a shriek. She wouldn't buy that, not a chance. And, truth be told, neither did I.

I hated to disappoint her. Like a lot of people, I had always sought my mother's approval. And, for the most part, I'd had it: I'd done well at school; achieved good A levels; almost finished my degree and I had even managed to pass the elusive driving test. But Jake was a different story. He had always been a bone of contention between us. 'He is too old for you' she would say, 'not good enough'. I could feel tears starting to well in the corners of my eyes. I wished she would say something. I wished she would tell me that everything would be ok and that seeing him again wasn't a terrible lapse in judgement. She didn't. There was only silence.

I blinked hard in an attempt to keep the tears from escaping down my face. This was silly; I was an adult and I could date whoever I wanted. It was my life and I had to make my own decisions now. Trying to break the silence, I started to sing along to the tinny sounding song on the radio. Immediately, I felt a pang of guilt; the quiet was more appropriate.

Finally, after just over two hours, we approached the car park at the seafront near 'our' ice cream shop. We had always come to this ice cream shop as the first port of call on our holidays. At home, our entire staircase was covered with pictures of me at varying ages clutching the remnants of half-eaten ice creams outside this very shop. It stood alone on the seafront and the old, metal sign creaked precariously above the door.

I manoeuvred into a parking space, checking my mirrors diligently. It wasn't really necessary as the car park was deserted save one lonely car. As I clambered out of the car, I felt the tension start to dissipate from my shoulders. The expanse of sky and sea that greeted my eyes was a welcome relief. I breathed deeply letting the air expand my lungs as far as they would go. Stretching out my arms to the sky, I felt acutely alive. My senses were alert and the smell of the doughnuts from the ice cream shop mixed with the sea salt was intoxicating. "We're here mum!" The corners of my mouth twitched and instinctively my hand flew to my mouth as if keeping something trapped inside.

Mablethorpe was still half asleep at this time of year; it would be another month or so before it roared into life. I was glad to have 'our' ice cream shop and 'our' spot on the beach to ourselves. And I knew my mum would be too. She didn't really like it when throngs of people migrated to the beach on hot days and littered the sands with pop cans and discarded bread crusts. That's why we usually came in June, before the schools broke up for the summer and a tirade of holiday makers invaded the town.

Luckily, the ice cream shop wasn't perturbed by the empty beach and remained open all year round. The old shop keeper had once told my mum that they did a little bit of catering for parties which kept them going out of season. She would always spend a while chatting to him; by the time she returned with the ice creams, they had already started to run down the sides of the cone. When I was young, it used to annoy me and I would say she could 'talk the hind leg off a donkey'. I mulled that phrase over in my mind for a moment before I opened the door to the shop. I turned to tell her what a funny old phrase it was. But stopped. Maybe this wasn't the time.

Hearing the familiar chime of the door, I stepped into the compact shop. The whole of the counter was a big fridge displaying an array of coloured ice creams.

"Hi there Georgia," the proprietor smiled a toothless grin.

My mum always said it was probably too much ice cream that had rotted his teeth. I smiled at the thought as I perused the offerings.

"A little early in the year for you isn't it? Usually June?"

I nodded without taking my eyes off the ice cream.

"I've just passed my test." I replied. Polite but not wanting to engage him much in further conversation.

It didn't take me long to choose mum's; she always had the same: chocolate orange with chocolate chips. I was a little more adventurous.

"Hmmmm, what is that one?" I pointed at a beige coloured ice cream with brown chunks in.

"It's rum and raisin, new this year that one."

I could almost taste it in my mouth. I was suddenly aware of how hungry I was. I couldn't really remember the last time I had eaten.

"I'll have that one."

"Right you are."

He scooped the ice cream and held it out to me offering me a final gummy smile as I turned to the door.

I took the ice cream out to the beach where I had left mum and my bag. I sat and looked at the sea, licking my ice cream with relish. It was calm; I was glad about that. Hanging low in the sky, the sun cast a watery light over the beach. The sea and the sand looked almost silver. Serene. Casting my eyes in both directions, the only other soul I spotted on the sand was the silhouette of a lone dog walker throwing a stick for a dog almost half the size of the man.

"I wonder who is taking who for a walk?" I joked.

The powder blue sky stretched out infinitely with only the occasional cloud to punctuate it. If it wasn't so chilly, I could almost imagine it was a summer's day. I pictured 21 happy holidays in my mind one after the other and smiled.

Eventually, after elongating the process, I finished my ice cream and turned to my mum,

"Are you ready?"

Carefully, I rolled up my trouser legs and took off my shoes and socks. I left them abandoned beside the shop. It was tradition that we always dipped our toes in the sea. My toes almost curled at the thought of it; I imagined the shock from the icy water and shuddered. I padded along the sand until I reached the water's edge. Wet sand clung to my feet and felt like soggy Weetabix between my toes. Reaching out one foot tentatively towards the water, I wrapped my arms carefully around my precious cargo. I didn't want to let go. I let out an audible gasp as my foot made contact with the glacial sea. Cold ricochet up my body like a lightning bolt. I wondered if perhaps today wasn't the right day; I thought maybe it was too cold. Even the tears tracing the contours of my face felt frozen.

I was just putting it off. The feeling of the hard metal in my hands was the only warmth I had left. With numb lips, I kissed the top of it. There was nowhere else she would rather be; I knew that. Slowly, I opened the urn and started to let her ashes fall into the murky water.

"I told you I would take you to Mablethorpe in my car eventually didn't I?" I whispered.

I felt her voice in the wind, "I never doubted you."

THE RIVER CHILDREN
by
Penny Rogers

Lauren cried all the way home from school. Manda's voice rang in her ears, the words so shrill they hurt her head. With her eyes and nose running uncontrollably and a vinegary taste in her mouth she just wanted to get into the house and up to her bedroom without being heard. Usually that was easy but today nothing had gone right, so she supposed that her aunt would be waiting for her by the back door.

'Your dad was sent to prison, your dad killed your mum. Your dad was sent to prison, your dad killed.....' Manda's high metallic voice echoed around her head. It wasn't true, it couldn't be true. Or could it? She remembered hitting Manda hard. Her blow stopped the taunts, but they were replaced by screams, and more blood than Lauren had ever seen. Someone got Mrs Cummings. Lauren knew she was in trouble. Big trouble.

The house was quiet; Lauren crept up to her room. Uncle Ray was still at work, Auntie Chris was watching television. Lauren could hear the music for 'Flog It!' Stupid programme, stupid music but Auntie Chris loved it. Safe in her room Lauren cried some more. Then quite suddenly she stopped. She had to find out the truth.

Auntie Chris and Uncle Ray had always told her that her mummy was dead. They said that she had an accident when Lauren was a baby. She had a photo of her mum, smiling and with brown hair just like

Lauren's, but she had no idea whether her dad was tall or short, fat or thin, fair or dark. No one ever mentioned her father. Just that he had had to go away and that one day he might come back to see her. They'd say stuff like 'Don't let's talk about that. Come with Uncle Ray and pick some beans.' It made her angry; they should've told her the truth and not kept inventing distractions and changing the subject.

Would they be honest with her now? She was after all eleven years old. Not a baby any more. She wondered about asking her cousin Joel; he was seventeen, and a grown-up. But no, he wouldn't tell her anything, he was only interested in football and his Xbox, though she had seen him walking up the High Street holding Lola Gooding's hand. As she washed her face she decided to ask Joel about her mum and dad, and if he wouldn't tell her anything she'd make him. She'd overheard her aunt and uncle talking about Lola Gooding, using words like 'trouble' and 'bad influence'. She thought Lola was cool, with her funky red hair and tattoos, but she had a good idea that Joel would not want his mum and dad knowing he was holding hands with her.

Feeling much calmer now she had a plan, Lauren changed into her jeans and her camouflage top. She put on her grippiest shoes. Downstairs she could hear the 'Flog It!' presenter in full flow. Now was the time to get out of the house. As she was creeping down the stairs the phone rang. She heard Auntie Chris answer it.

'Oh Mrs Cummings, is everything alright?'

For the second time that day she tasted vinegar. Throwing caution to the wind she ran down the stairs and out of the house. As she reached the end of the garden she heard her aunt's voice calling urgently

'Come back Lauren. I need to talk to you.'

Lauren didn't stop running until she knew no one would find her. The woods that bordered the garden had been her playground for years. She knew every path, every tree, and every bit of tangled undergrowth. She knew where to find wood anemones and bluebells in the spring, hazelnuts in the late summer and holly in the winter. She knew where the boggy bits were, she knew where the long-hidden barbed wire protruded from under a blanket of leaves. She felt safe in the woods.

The oak tree with a branch broken so that it touched the ground was her favourite place. And it was here that she went to think. She climbed the familiar branch, gripping the deeply grained bark with her shoes all the while listening to the messages rustling through the leaves. 'He's in prison Lauren' the leaves told her. So it must be true. Her dad had killed her mum. Murdered her. He was in prison and since she had hurt Manda badly she might be sent to prison as well. Mrs Cummings had rung Auntie Chris; she was in such trouble. Salty tears ran once more down her puffy cheeks.

The trees changed their words to her. She stopped crying and listened carefully. The branches creaked and groaned; the leaves rustled a new rhythm as if they were practising saying something. After a while she began to make sense of their words.

'Find the River Children. Find the River Children.' Lauren knew exactly what they meant.

The boundary between the woods and the moorland beyond was marked by a stream. Not a large stream for most of the year, although in winter it filled up and became almost a river. Even in the driest summers there were pools, some very small, hidden deep within the rocks. She had heard and seen the River Children here. A girl dressed in really old fashioned clothes with a scarf on her head and no shoes, and a boy with no clothes at all. He was very thin. His ribs stuck out and his skin was covered in cuts and bruises. She had heard a baby crying and a girl calling. Once she had heard a dog barking.

Slowly she made her way towards the edge of the trees. She heard the leaves settling down as the breeze dropped. They sighed at her.

'Good journey' they said. 'Sleep well.'

By the stream all was quiet. There was no sign of the River Children. Lauren poked the gravelly edge of the water with a stick. She didn't want to go back to her aunt and uncle. She didn't want to see Joel or Mrs Cummings and especially not Manda ever again.

As she turned round she noticed a movement so faint that she wondered if it was a shadow. She stared at the spot where she had seen the flicker. As she watched a girl appeared. It was the girl she had seen before, dressed in a brown smock of some really rough material, a cream scarf over her head and no shoes on her feet. The girl beckoned. Lauren stood rooted to the spot. She knew she should go home. But where was home? What lies and half truths were waiting for her at her aunt and uncle's house? What would happen at school? Hesitantly she left her poking stick and followed the girl.

As she walked up the stream she noticed the water getting deeper and the pools looked almost black. Beyond the hills the sun started to go down. Lauren knew she ought to turn back, but she kept going. She realised the girl was no longer alone. A scruffy little dog was trotting by her heels and ahead of her the naked boy ran and threw stones into the water. She could clearly see the dreadful cuts and bruises on his emaciated body; she shuddered wondering what had happened to him. Then she heard the baby crying. She supposed someone was carrying it.

She called out 'Who are you? Where are we going?'

But there was no answer, just an encouraging gesture from the girl in brown. She realised that another girl was walking by her side. Lauren looked at her. She must be about the same age as me, she mused, but how does she walk in all those stiff clothes? The girl marched effortlessly over the uneven ground, and with a gasp Lauren realised that she could see the outline of the now distant woods through the girl's tight jacket.

She thought about Auntie Chris and Uncle Ray. They would be very worried about her and they'd always tried to be kind to her. But they weren't her mum and dad, and they should've told her about what had happened to her parents. She considered her blackmail plan and decided that it wouldn't work; neither would it be fair to Joel who was mostly nice to her, or indeed fair to Lola Gooding who was just so cool. She wondered about her dad, the man she had known nothing about until today. He'd killed her mum and she wanted to know why. She needed to know if he loved her; there were so many questions jostling in her head. If she turned round now she might be able to find out about what had happened. Then she remembered Mrs Cummings and the phone call that had made her run away. In her mind's eye she saw Manda and all the blood. Perhaps Manda was dead! The vinegar taste rose once more in her mouth. She turned away from the sight of the far-off woods and began to cry.

The River Children gathered round Lauren. For the first time she felt a hand on her shoulder, it was the emaciated boy who pointed to the stream where the rays of the dying sun lit the edge of the pool. Lauren looked back at the woods. Auntie Chris and Uncle Ray would be looking for her, and she turned round just enough to see the path back down the stream. But the water looked inviting, infinitely more so than the thought of school and much more welcoming than Auntie Chris's house and the trouble in store for her there. The girl in brown smiled and took her hand. She understands, thought Lauren, she'll be my sister and this will be my new family. She thought about her unknown father. He had killed her mum, murdered her. Lauren shuddered as she realised the she would never want to meet the man who had done that, even if he was her dad. She moved a step closer towards the deep and dark water. Calmly and carefully she picked her way over the stones. She could see that the girl in tight clothes was now carrying the baby. It had stopped crying and was fast asleep in the girl's arms. Eight or ten children of various ages gathered round her. They were all dressed in unusual clothes; a bit like those in an illustration in a book on the history of fashion that she had looked at in the library. Some held out their hands to her, one of the little ones grabbed the hem of her camouflage top. She thought she might have heard her name being called, carried from far away on the evening breeze. Around her heels the scruffy dog ran about, yapping with excitement. If he was real he'd trip me up thought Lauren. The River Children closed in around her. For a short time she hesitated, then followed her new family into the sanctuary of the deep water.

RUGGED

by

Douglas Murdoch

I didn't catch your name the first time you said it to me, but I nodded anyway because I didn't want you to think I didn't care. The music was loud and the bass was beating down on my skull – I swear it was doing damage. But you were there and something felt different, so I stayed.

I didn't speak to you again that night. Not for lack of trying, might I add. I looked for you – I really did – but you'd left the club for bigger and better things by the time I'd plucked up the courage to ask you, well, anything.

The second time I spoke to you was at the bus stop. I'd just finished work and it was late; dark clouds blotted the starry sky, and a chill had whipped up in the air. The bus was late, which was convenient for you, because you turned up slightly after it was due, tipsy and gorgeous. You said you recognised me. I explained how we'd been out the week before and then we got to chatting. You spent quite a while complaining about your ex, who I guess must have been both a complete dick and, all things considered, entirely blind, because you said he cheated on you. I remember finding it hard to imagine how someone could find anyone more worthy to spend their time on than you.

We got on the bus together and you fell asleep on my shoulder. You looked so peaceful, which made it hard to wake you when my stop arrived. But you sleepily acknowledged my departure with a gentle smile.

It was a Thursday when we spoke for the third time. I remember because I was working at the pub and, by that point, I was only working Thursdays and Fridays. You walked in with a bunch of your friends – friends who, whilst attractive, paled in comparison to you. I remember realising at this point how incredibly out of my league you were – I was pale, spotty, unshaven, with messy hair that a comb could not tame. You? You were angelic.

But maybe you took pity on me, because you sat perched on a barstool across from me for most of the night. I was thankful that it was quiet that night – I was able to actually talk to you without too many interruptions, even if I did stumble over my words. But you took it in your stride; you smiled, you laughed, you started up conversation when words failed me, as they so often did in your presence. And frankly, you overwhelmed me. You stayed until the pub closed that night, and it was only after I'd shut it all up and was ready to leave that I realised you'd waited for me. Your friends had gone and it was just you and me.

I asked you why you waited for me and you said you realised you forgot something.

And then you kissed me.

Wow.

The fourth time was just you and me. I invited you out for coffee. You talked a lot more than me but I was glad about that, because you'd already told me a full story by the time I was able to get past the nerves

41

to string a coherent sentence together. I remember that at one point, my hand was on the table and you placed yours on it, softly stroking my skin with your thumb. It was just a little action, but it was enough to confirm to me that I liked this. I liked you. You invited me round to yours later, and said goodbye with a kiss.

When I got to yours that evening, all we did was watch TV, but it was perfect. It was halfway through some crappy American sitcom that you kissed me again – and this one lasted for longer. When you pulled away, you smiled. Your eyes rested on mine and we looked into each other for a few minutes, trading emotions, sharing secrets, sending words through our eyes we'd never let leave our lips. I stayed over that night, and I slept with my arms wrapped around you.

Your flatmate was there the fifth time we met. Her name was Justine and she was nice – we got on well. She said you'd made a good choice with me and that (God knows why) she approved of the "rugged" kind of look I was modelling. It wasn't a look I was aiming for, but it required no effort, so I took the compliment, rather happy that my scruffy style now had a more appealing name. After that, you kept calling me Rugged – it basically became my new pet-name. I'm not sure how I felt about that, but you were gorgeous, and you were mine, so I couldn't complain.

The sixth and seventh times we met were in Octavia Park. The first time we just walked along the river, had an ice cream, and tried to avoid getting rained on. The second time we set out a picnic on the grass – and again, tried to avoid getting rained on.

Neither went to plan – both went much better. Soggy sandwiches under a not-too-sheltered tree turned out to be much better than sun. It was stupid and beautiful – us two, fiercely set on having a day out in the park as the rain soaked us to the bone; I think I laughed more that day than I ever have.

On the eighth time, you texted me saying you were upset and I was round yours as soon as I could be. When the door was pulled open, you told me I didn't need to come over – you were fine. I told you I didn't care. Five minutes later you were sobbing on my shoulder. You explained that some days you just got like this – you just got sad. You told me it used to happen about once a week. You told me this was the first time it'd happened since we met. I held you closer, and soon the tears stopped. It sounds terrible, but I loved that night. I saw you. I properly saw you. When you had no words left, you spoke so much louder. I saw flaws, faults, scars, jagged edges – and I saw how you were dealing with them, how they weren't hidden away. And I respected you so much.

The ninth time we met, we went out with my friend, Jake, and his girlfriend. I remember being so proud to show you off – yes, this one's mine! Yes, really! *I know!* We had a nice meal despite conversation being almost entirely centralised around Anna, Jake's girlfriend, because Anna enjoyed talking about Anna. A lot. The evening dragged on as we heard about Anna and Anna and more Anna.

When you and I went home, we spent the rest of the night jokily complaining about her. Your impression was flawless, but you always impersonated her narcissistic tones with a blush. You didn't want to be rude – or mean. You were very conscious that you might be meeting her several times in the future, considering how close I was to Jake. Turns out that wouldn't be an issue; Jake and Anna broke up two days later.

The tenth time we met, I started losing count. Days with you blurred into one perfect experience; days without you turned into non-events. We'd chat every day online. Every night, you'd end your texts with "*Love you, Rugged. Love you quite a bit.*" And always with six kisses. Never more, never less. Always six. I'd look forward to counting them every night – counting those six kisses that reminded me how lucky I was that they were for me. That you were mine.

The final time I saw you went too quickly.

We were at the pub – the pub where you kissed me – where I used to work. Cringey 80s music was being vomited by the jukebox, courtesy of a drunken group of middle-age men. It was terrible music, and we grumbled about it a lot, but every now and then we'd catch ourselves humming along and we'd share a grin. By the time we'd had a few pints, we were singing along to each song as it arrived, laughing and jarringly moving in a way we called dancing. It was you, me, Jake and another of my friends called Sara.

We had a laugh, that night. We really did. I remember leaving you at the doorstep. I said you should come round mine, but you had work in the morning so you decided against it.

You kissed me. I kissed you back. And then you walked off, waving a little as you did. You looked amazing in the moonlight.

You *were* amazing.

I loved you.

It was 5:32am when I got the call.

I was practically asleep, but then they said your name and asked if I knew you and I said yes. And suddenly I was awake because they were saying these things, these impossible *wrong* things and they were asking when I last saw you and they were trying to work out who did it and the neighbours had heard cries of *fag!* and punches and there was blood too much blood and no no *no!*

No.

No...

You would've hated your funeral. It was solemn and full of tears. You didn't want to go this way. You wanted glitter and smiles, but no, there you were − in a box, surrounded by broken shards of people who were trying to accept that you weren't there anymore.

The police said it was probably a hate crime. A homophobic attack. They haven't found the people who did it yet. But they will. I swear to God, I'll make sure they will.

You were twenty years old.

You still are twenty years old.

You'll always be twenty years old because those boys couldn't accept it. Those boys with their knives and their hoods up and their cries of *fag! fag!* couldn't accept that a boy could love a boy, and that

that could be okay. That you could love me, and that that could be okay. That it could be more than okay – that it could be the best goddamned thing that ever happened to me, that it could make me feel like I could do anything that it could make me feel like the stars were mine and the sun was ours and that everything was going to be okay even if it didn't seem that way and that everything was okay as long as we were together that nothing mattered but you that nothing mattered *but you* why couldn't they understand it *why could they understand?!*

Why?

Why…?

I don't know.

I miss you.

I miss you so much.

I wish I could kiss you six times.

EGO, I
by
Harriet Avery

He saw tree trunks striped vertically; pale shapes of sky taut between the branches; orange ferns at knee-height; wind like water above his head; birdsong.

He had no idea where he was.

His head pounded. This made no sense. Why was he here? There must have been some kind of accident. He was upright – but his lungs seemed to be constricting – he sucked oxygen – the world span – it was all he could do to remain on his feet. Around him, the forest rustled and nodded impenetrably. His eyes searched, but he recognised – nothing.

There must have been some kind of accident.

He stepped forward. Shivers bounced through the ferns underfoot – something flew from a branch. Twigs and needles spiralled, a disintegrating shower marking the invisible flight. And then he saw the car, bent around the tree.

He stared at it for a long while. It was half-submerged; the bonnet, crunched around the unyielding trunk, almost invisible under the brambles. Pieces of metal sprouted from the forest floor, jutting between the leaves. Only the rear wheels were exposed, trailing deep red ruts in the churned earth.

He waited for recognition to kick in. He knew what the badge meant – it was a Mercedes; a C-class model. But the numbers and letters on the number plate were entirely unfamiliar.

It occurred to him that he might be hurt. He looked down at himself, a swooping sensation looping through his stomach. With a certain amount of relief, he could see no immediate sign of any injury: all his limbs, present and correct, with a reassuring lack of blood. He touched his head carefully, and then put out his hands, examining the crevices criss-crossing his palms, his life-line, his heart-line, his marriage-line.

Although, actually, he didn't know if he was married. He stopped, and frowned. Did he have a wife? He thought about it. That was really something he ought to know. No face came to mind, but he felt no certainty that he was unmarried.

This worried him. How could he not know?

The answer was obvious. He knew it before he was prepared to admit it. He had woken, confused, following a car accident. Something had obviously happened to his memory.

There must have been some kind of accident.

He took several deep breaths. 'Ok,' he said. 'Ok.' This made him feel better. He needed to hear a voice – he needed to hear his own voice. He needed to hear his own voice saying his own name: 'You're ok – ' he said again – but the void behind his eyes, in his brain, intruded like the shutting of a door. He pushed through blank jigsaw pieces with increasing desperation. No name rose to his tongue. Nothing.

Panic engulfed him. He ripped through the undergrowth. The driver's door gaped. He found a wallet in the clutter. Inside: a driving license.

There, printed, was his name. Phillip James Gillings. He ran his finger over the thumbnail photograph and the handwritten signature, feeling his chest deflate, the tightening subside. Yes, there were the words he'd written and supplied. He leant back, and spoke his name aloud.

The name felt strange. He did not recognise it. Fervently ignoring this, he flipped through the wallet, discovering a photograph in the card-holder. On the back were scribbled words: *Helen & Joy*. He sat in the driver's seat, looking at the photo. The dark-haired woman had her cheek pressed to the baby's forehead. She had grey pimpled smudges of tiredness under her eyes. The baby was pudgy and plain. He felt as little attachment to them as to the wooden banisters behind them in the background.

The rest of the contents of the glove compartment had spilled out. Papers fanned across the floor-mat, an incomprehensible table of numbers and codes. He leaned across and shuffled through the pages. The grid continued, apparently without change, on and on, pages and pages. The same blue logo headed each new page: *Hewitt&Devlin LLP*. This must be his job.

He pushed them aside, and picked up a paperback book. *The Aeneid.* He opened it at a page marked with a receipt. *Infandum, regina, iubes renouare dolorem,* he read incomprehensibly. Perhaps he'd forgotten how to read, he thought with desperate hilarity. He flipped through more pages. There was a glossary at the back: *ego, is, ea, id*, he read; *(nominative), I, he, she, it.* He threw it down: the English pronouns were as unhelpful as the Latin. He examined the receipt: it recorded the purchase of Wine-Gums, Horlicks and a birthday card. It was dated 07/07/2016, from a Tesco in somewhere called Trimley. He wondered where that was. He emptied a capsule of Tic-Tacs into his hand. The tiny plastic pills trickled across his palm. He couldn't bring himself to swallow one.

At length, he ran out of things to reboot his memory. Slowly, he climbed from the wrecked car. Getting out of the car was worse than finding himself next to it. He felt that he could remember, dimly, a black explosion; the breaking of undergrowth; the judder of tyres as he lost control. It played like a silent film in his head.

The only sensible course of action seemed to be to follow the tyre-treads grooved deep into the ground and retrace his way back to civilisation. The treads were scars in the dirt, furrows carved into the broken ferns.

He almost stepped on it – on the ground, a rectangular gleam of reflected light. A mobile phone.

After some muddling, he found the name *Helen* in the Contacts list. The phone rang five times. An unfamiliar female voice answered: 'Phil?'

'Helen?' he said. 'Helen. Listen, I'm fine, but I've had –'

'Phil? Is that you? You sound weird.'

'Helen – I've – I think I've lost –' It suddenly seemed foolish to say it. It was ridiculous. Embarrassing.

'Look, is it important, Phil? I'm working,' she interrupted. 'You could ring Joy, you know. If you can make time in your oh-so-busy schedule.'

He was puzzled. The image of the baby in the photograph floated in his mind. 'But Joy –' he stammered. 'Wait, how old is Joy?'

A frosty silence followed. 'Yeah, I've been wondering how long it would take you. She was nineteen, Phil. *Last week.*'

With a sudden jerk, he hung up. He wanted to throw the phone down, and back away from it.

He dialled nine-nine-nine. The police dispatcher was brisk and efficient. 'We received a call from this number ten minutes ago. Are you the same caller?'

He was thrown by this unexpected question. She took his hesitation as confirmation.

'Sir, the team *are* on their way. I'll stay on the line with you, if you don't hang up. The address of the emergency is still outside St Benedict's?'

'I don't know.' He began to walk along the tyre marks. 'I'm – I'm having some trouble remembering things.' The ground sloped upwards, his feet pushing into the loose soil and crushed leaves.

He heard rapid clicking. 'OK, it seems you mentioned a head injury…' He crested the incline, feeling his head with his hand. It felt ok. Ahead, beyond thinning trees, and a stretch of concrete, there was a large red-brick building. He hurried towards it.

'Can you tell me if you are experiencing any difficulty in seeing, Mr Gillings?'

'No.'

He stepped out from the trees, and stood in the centre of a deserted road, which curved away from him on both sides. Ahead was the building, looming behind metal railings. There was a gate, which was wide open. For the first time, he felt as if these things, and their presence in this particular place, right there in front of him, made some sort of sense. He seemed to have expected it. It was familiar.

'And have you felt nauseous, or been sick at all? Can you describe the location of any pain?'

'No…'

He answered the dispatcher's routine questions, searching the imposing building with his eyes. He was oddly unwilling to enter through the gate. He peered up and down the road.

'Excuse me!'

A new voice called to him. There was a woman coming towards him from the building, dressed in purple scrubs. He began to back away into the forest, and then stopped, confused.

'You look lost. St Benedict's Hospital?' she said.

He didn't understand, so he said nothing.

'Don't worry, we get loads turning off too early, and getting lost here,' she said. 'If you follow the road round, you do reach the entrance eventually.'

She closed the gate, drawing the bolt across. 'I would let you in this way, but we're on security alert right now, and I'd get into trouble.'

'Oh.' He didn't know why he didn't ask her for help.

'Someone has wandered off from Psych apparently – nightmare…' she threw up her hands in a gesture of frustration. 'Not my ward, thank goodness… Anyway, I'd get yourself to reception asap, ok? They'll give you a visitor pass.' She walked away, back into her own world, tutting at the incompetence of security guards.

He watched her disappear.

'Hello? Hello?' The police dispatcher was still on the other end on the phone.

'Hello – did you hear that?' he said.

'Yes – you *are* outside St Benedict's.' More clicking from her end. 'Ok, Mr Gillings, can I suggest you follow her advice and head to the hospital reception? The unit are on their way, so they will sort your car, and I'll tell them to find you in the hospital. It sounds like you should get yourself some medical assistance.'

'Ok,' he said, and ended the call. He stood for a while in the road, hesitating. Then he turned round and heading back into the dark of the forest. He could not bring himself to go into the hospital, although he was unsure why. He felt a distinct relief to be retreating from the redbrick building.

As he descended the slope, something emerged in the leaves at the corner of his eye. He stopped, his heart leaping into his throat. It was a dark shape prone in the ferns. After a moment, he went towards it, cautiously. As it became clearer, he stopped.

It was a man. He was lying on the ground, on his back, with blood running down his head. The blood was astonishingly bright against his white skin.

This was some kind of waking nightmare. He knelt beside the man, feeling dizzy with horror. He tried to make himself breathe slowly; his lungs were squeezing themselves tighter and tighter.

The ground was damp; the ferns rose up to his throat. He touched the man's face with a fingertip, avoiding the blood. The skin was cold and prickled with stubble. He stood up, and looked down at him, wondering what to do. He couldn't call the police again. He wanted to retch – to recoil – to run – but instead, he reached down, and awkwardly, with a heave, he rolled the stranger onto his side, aiming for the recovery position.

The man flopped, heavy and limp. Something fell out of his pocket. The blood began to dribble sideways across the fleshy cheek, leaving crimson tracks like tyre marks.

Looking at that pale face, it suddenly struck him that he *knew* this man. Or not quite *knew*, exactly – it was just that his face was unexpectedly familiar. Those wide cheeks, the wrinkles across the forehead. The groove between the eyebrows. That mole by the left eye.

There must have been some kind of accident.

He had seen that face before. He knew it, with a cold certainty. Where had he seen it? Did he know this man? He thought, no, he didn't. It was just that face. Nothing more.

It filtered through his muddled head. He recognised the face – only the face. As if from a photograph. It *was* from a photograph. A thumbnail photograph. On a driver's license.

His heart pounding, he grabbed the object which had fallen from the stranger's pocket, and looked at it. It was a lanyard pass. Its cord still looped the stranger's neck. It was printed with two things: a name, and the blue logo of *Hewitt&Devlin*. He read the name.

He straightened slowly, letting the lanyard slip from shaking hands. Now he understood. Now he knew. Now his fear of St Benedict's hospital made sense.

The name of man on the ground was Phillip Gillings.

Mr. POLLOCK'S BICYCLE
by
Christine Griffin

He hadn't meant to scare the child, but it was nothing new. Most children screamed when they saw him. That's why he kept himself to himself as much as possible. All his life he'd walked in the shadows, creeping along the margins of life. He'd shuffle to the Post Office occasionally or to the corner shop before it was properly light then slip back home before anyone could see him.

'Out of sight, out of mind, ' his Aunt Kath used to say when she shoved him in the cupboard under the stairs. 'You're not fit to be seen by decent folks.'

Mr Pollock had lived for decades keeping out of sight. Out of mind was easy since no-one knew or cared about him anyway.

Until now that is - a bright day in May in the fifty- fifth year of his life when everything changed. For on this day, Mr Pollock found himself in the grip of a longing so deep that he left his house, in broad daylight, crossed the road and knocked on the door of number 17.

Of course the child had screamed when his father answered the door. Anyone would scream at the sight of him.

He remembered his Aunt Edna's comment on his six-year old self- 'Looks like one of those gargoyle things on churches.' And worse, his Aunt Kath - 'Midwife should have put a pillow over it at birth.'

He remembered his soft, lavender-scented mother saying, 'Reginald's got a lovely nature. That's what counts.'

His other aunt, Aunt Izzie had snorted, 'As if anyone cares about that.'

'Can I help you, pal?' The man from number 17 put the child down and was staring at Mr Pollock.

'Er yes.' He wasn't used to speaking out loud and his voice was raspy and coarse. 'I was wondering...' He pointed to the skip in front of the house. 'The bicycle'. The words in his mouth felt strange and marvellous, like a magical incantation. He pointed again. 'The bicycle.'

The man from number 17 stepped outside. 'Yeah. Getting rid of it. Got a new one now. State of the art.'

Mr Pollock reached up and stroked the wheel. 'I was wondering...'

'What - you want this old thing do you?'

Mr Pollock nodded. The man from number 17 looked at him in disbelief, but there was no mistaking the earnestness of the strange man on his doorstep.

'Tell you what, pal - give us a week or so and I'll clean it up for you. Pop back then.'

Back home, Mr Pollock paced the floor. A week or so. Seven days. Seven days and he'd be the owner of a bike. Since he was a young lad, he'd longed for one. All the kids in his street had bikes, but no one ever offered him a go. He was too strange, too ugly. And it was no use asking Aunt Kath. When his mother died, Aunt Kath had done her duty and taken him in, but that was as far as it went. In all her life, she never showed him one act of kindness. She never called him by his name and never gave him anything. Not even on his birthday or at Christmas. The dog fared better than he did.

From his window, Mr Pollock watched the man from number 17 lift the bike down and take it into the house. Please don't change your mind, he thought. Don't decide you want to keep it after all.

Six days, and twenty three hours later, he left his house and crossed the road. He was just about to ring, when the door opened and the man came out. He had the child with him and oddly enough it wasn't screaming this time. Just staring.

'There you go, pal. Cleaned up and oiled, ready to go.'

Mr Pollock was overcome. The rusty dilapidated bike had gone. In its place was a thing of wonder, blue and silver, shining in the sun. He reached out and caressed the saddle. 'Thank you,' he said, the unfamiliar words clumsy on his tongue.

'Anytime, pal. Give us a shout if you need anything.'

Pal. How strange. As if the man actually liked him. As if he didn't see his ugly twisted face. As if he, Mr Pollock, was just any old guy walking along the street. He wheeled his new possession back home, his heart fluttering with excitement.

For a week, the bike took pride of place in Mr Pollock's sitting room. Each day he took a cloth and dusted it, marvelling at the gears, the glittering spokes, the shiny bell. It was the only thing he'd ever yearned for in his whole life – well apart from having a normal face and people to talk to, but he'd given up on those years ago.

Eddie Hawkins' bike had been red. The memory of that day still stabbed him in the stomach. Eddie's dad had knocked on Aunt Kath's door holding the red bike.

'Thought your lad might like it,' he'd said. 'Too small for our Eddie now. You can have it for nowt.'

Mr Pollock remembered crouching in the hallway willing her with all his heart to say yes.

'He's not my lad and I'm not having your cast-offs,' Aunt Kath said. 'Anyway, he's not fit to be seen outside. Give it to the rag and bone man. And get off my clean step.'

Eight days after he'd crossed the road for the second time and collected the bicycle, Mr Pollock got up very early. He made himself a cup of tea and stared at the bike. Then he put on his coat, pulled his on his balaclava and pushed the bike towards the park. Time he learned how to ride, he decided, winding a scarf around his neck.

A few dog walkers were about and once they were out of sight Mr Pollock mounted the bike and wobbled a few feet before falling off. The lads in his childhood street had made it look so easy. Doing wheelies, Eddie Hawkins had called it. He righted the bike and this time pedalled a good twenty feet before falling off.

The youths appeared from nowhere, slouching their way to school, smoking and looking for trouble. Mr Pollock was just remounting to have another go when he heard their mocking laughter. Then one of the boys threw a stone. It hit him on his temple and he fell to the ground. Unable to get up, he watched as they kicked his bike and stamped on it, laughing and jeering. Then while a couple of them heaved what was left of the bike into the boating lake, one of them aimed a couple of vicious kicks at his head before they all ran off laughing.

When he came round, he was aware of a sea of faces looking down on him and a babble of outraged voices. Then one voice detached itself from the rest.

'It's ok. I'll see to this. He's from my street.' A strong arm eased itself under his neck. 'It's alright, pal, I've got you. Let's get you fixed up eh, shall we.'

Mr Pollock hadn't cried since he was a child. He'd learned long ago that it got him nowhere, made matters worse in fact. But now hot tears flowed down his face biting into his cuts. A woman reached down to him with a handful of tissues and the tears flowed even more, gathering into huge shuddering sobs. Decades of misery and neglect flowed down his ugly deformed face, and all because a man had called him 'pal' and a woman was mopping his face with tissues.

'What's your name, love?' It was the tissue woman, crouched down beside him.

'Mr Pollock,' he gulped through his sobs.

'No, your first name.'

'First name?' He paused, remembering his mother. 'Reginald's got a lovely nature'.

'Mother used to call me Reginald.'

'Well how about that,' said the man from number 17. 'My mam always calls me Reggie, short for Reginald. A real man's name that is.'

The crowd murmured its approval. Two of them were fishing the battered bike out of the lake, muttering about axles and gears. A ripple spread through them as they heard an ambulance siren threading its way across town.

'Won't be long now, pal. I'm going with you and when they've fixed you up, you're coming back to mine for a cuppa. The missus'll never forgive me if I don't so no arguments.'

The paramedic slipped a needle into his arm and Mr Pollock drifted into a pleasant trance. He wondered what it would feel like to go into number 17 and have a cuppa. As if he wasn't an ugly misfit, a church gargoyle hiding from the world, but an ordinary person, drinking tea with his neighbours like anyone else.

Maybe they'd talk about bikes. Or the little boy. Or the weather.

And maybe they'd just drink tea.

BEAUTIFUL FEET
by
Sue Mays

We're rehearsing a play; well it's more of a love poem really. In fact it should really be done to music, but old Sol's singing voice isn't up to much - a bit of a handicap when he's got the starring role. He's also putting it about that he's written it. Actually I feel sorry for the CE - that's the Chief Eunuch, his secretary, who's really the one with the poetic turn of mind, although perhaps not so well equipped to deal with matters of love. Truth is old Sol has ideas, but not much idea of literature, so this is where I come in.

I'm the very tall one, standing in the background, holding a shepherd's crook and wearing a horrendous homespun tunic and oversized cheap sandals, while the 'Daughters of Jerusalem' in the chorus pretend not to smirk behind their veils. In Queenie's ledger I am number 27, but no-one's counting, except Queenie of course - she makes it her business to keep tabs on us all, as there are so many Rachels and Leahs and Jezebels, not to mention the weird foreign names. No-one except Queenie can keep up. I was part of a package deal with 26, my sister, the pretty one. Our father wanted rid and it made good sense to get us both into the royal collection when she caught the King's eye. Unfortunately she didn't survive long - the seniors saw to that, the Wives that is, but I found some favour as one of the few who could read and write. When Sol doesn't feel up to the other stuff he sends for me to read to him, or tell him a bedtime story.

So now here I am, a lovesick shepherd, sweating like a pig under the scratchy cloth, and having to prompt number 60, who is supposedly being wooed away from me by the King. She may be stunning and she's no doubt brilliant in bed, but born actress she is not. Perhaps I do her a disservice. She's hopeless at memorising lines, but she's pretty good at acting as far as old Sol's concerned. A country girl? Well she certainly wouldn't get far out in the fields in that silk chiffon, and she'll have to have dark face-paint on to give her anything like the right complexion. And as for her shoes, try stepping across the farmyard in those....

It was Sol who came up with the line 'How beautiful are thy feet in thy shoes, O Daughter of Princes', not bad really. But then there was another piece about breasts being like roes - absolute nonsense. Fish-eggs? More like poached hens eggs on this girl although she's still got some growing to do. I think there must have been a transcription error there, but he won't change it. 'Clusters of grapes' got through as well - not very flattering is it? I've managed to fix other things, on the quiet, as I've been drafted in on the re-write with the CE. I've slipped in lines like: 'How fair is thy love, my sister, my spouse'. I'm proud of that one as it does have a nice feel to it, and it reminds me of our family, before our father chose to break us all up.

Poor old Sol wanted a lot more stuff on feet (and shoes) because he's got a thing about them, but we persuaded him to tone it down as it's for the state visit next week, for the Queen of Sheba and her delegation. It wouldn't do to put *her* off, especially when he's hoping to make an impression with his kingly wisdom. So most of the waxing lyrical about feet has been cut now, although, sadly, not all of it.

Back to 60 then: she and her feet are a recent acquisition, still fresh as the morning dew, got promoted straight to junior wife even with her precious few connections. Not even a woman yet, often the case these days so he can get more usage. At least half the wives and concubines are 'resting' at any one time, pregnant, unclean or just ill. There has to be a regular throughput as so many disappear - what with the Fever, and childbirth, and sent away when they're barren, or not producing sons, or producing too many sons. And some just vanish. The constant supply of new young blood keeps old Sol happy, and his ministers usually make sure the goods come with dividends: trade treaties, foreign alliances and suchlike.

But I digress. To give her due credit, 60 is trying really hard with this play. Her outfit is stunning, awash with floaty fabrics and sparkling gemstones. Of course old Sol's pretty generous when he wants to be - it's common knowledge he's got plenty stashed away in the treasury. She's ordered special red satin shoes and had the heels built up with wooden blocks; she knows full well it does things to the shape of her legs.

At least Sol seems to think so, which is all that counts
- witness him drooling as he slips the shoes off her
feet, her beautiful feet. Poor kid. She must know that
number 61 will be along soon enough, and then
Jehovah help her. The Wives certainly won't.

Perhaps I should warn her about that other one,
my sister. She had lovely feet, such neat little toes with
perfect nails like tiny rose petals, and slim ankles to
die for, ravishing, with a simple gold chain on each
one. She spent hours polishing those nails with
perfumed oil, and rubbing away the dead skin on her
heels, and standing on tiptoe to strengthen her calf
muscles, ready for the dancing. She was a wonderful
dancer. But not for long. When the Wives had finished
with her she couldn't even walk. I never saw her feet
after that.

As for me, I'm pleased to say I'm still here
despite my obvious disadvantages. I've seen less of
old Sol at bedtime recently, since number 60's been in
action. The word out there is that 61 is almost in the
bag, at least if the play is a success with our visitor.
Not sure Queenie will approve though, as there can
only be one Number One, and the Sheba woman is
pretty feisty by the sound of it. I wonder whether she's
as good-looking as they make out. Perhaps she's really
tall and has big feet. There'd be some justice in that,
I'd like to think. A woman who can stand up on her
own two feet.

Meanwhile I'm looking forward to a sizeable
reward, some decent jewellery perhaps if it all works

out. Maybe some nice new shoes, with a bit of class, shoes that fit properly and make my legs look good, my feet less lumpy, for when I get invited to walk the Labyrinth again, to old Sol's lair I mean. But I don't mind too much about the bedtime stories, for the moment anyway. There's plenty to enjoy when the eunuchs aren't watching, and old Sol is worshipping all those beautiful little feet.

My last lines are coming up now. Thank Jehovah. Here's when I get to give up the girl, so old Sol can have his way. Good luck to him. I can finally slink off, dump the shepherd's crook, and grab a glass of mint tea in the shade. Perhaps I can crack a few jokes with the CE - if he's in the mood, and not fretting about the last scene.

60 is on her feet to the bitter end, of course. Poor kid. Act your socks off, is what I say, but you really need to watch where you walk on those beautiful feet.

4:45am, 4:48am, 4:56am and 4.59am

by

Warren Green

Maggie stared long and hard out of the kitchen window. Her tired, watery eyes focused on nothing particular outside in their overgrown garden. She wasn't wearing makeup and her long hair was unkempt, hiding most of her face. Her head was pounding as though she had a permanent migraine. She'd forgotten to take her medication again which didn't help with her feelings of anxiety and depression. She was getting more and more forgetful these days and the headaches were getting worse by the day. Maggie had also been unable to find the slip of paper where she'd written down the doctor's telephone number.

She took in a deep breath and remained in her robotic, trance-like state. The lukewarm, soapy water in the plastic washing up bowl splashed and sloshed about as her frail hands continued to scrub the pots and pans. Thin lines of white, crystal like bubbles flowed slowly between the linear channels in the stainless-steel sink drainer. Maggie's piercing, outward stare remained as her hand searched automatically, swilling around the stagnant water in the bowl, only to find it now empty, except of course for the solitary teaspoon. It was carefully cleaned and placed neatly with the rest of the dull cutlery.

Suddenly, her green eyes beamed open as she heard a soft cry from the speaker of a baby monitor, carefully positioned on the work surface next to her.

Hastily, she snapped off her discoloured, lemon rubber gloves and threw them onto the untidy dining table before heading off upstairs to the nursery.

Reaching their room Maggie's anxious eyes scanned her four angels carefully. Each one was sleeping silently and lay still in the shadowy space. Her panic turned to relief, realising they were just fine. As she stared at them lovingly, a memory of the terrible incident flashed through her mind, the miscarriage with her first born, Daniel. It all seemed such a long time ago now. She wiped away a solitary tear from her cheek, realising just how lucky she and her husband Arthur had been to have brought four healthy babies into the world. The doctors had told them it was impossible for her to have any more children. Maggie always knew she'd prove them all wrong. She smiled in the darkness.

She saw a slight movement of Bethany and Gemma beneath their soft, pink blankets and knew it was almost their feeding time. They were always the hungriest of the four and knew she'd have to prepare their bottles in advance or face their wrath. It was also time for Arthur's morning cup of tea. Nice and strong, splash of milk and one and a half sugars. Any other way and he'd be grumpy for the rest of the day.

She headed off back downstairs to the kitchen to prepare their bottles and Arthur's tea. Arthur didn't like to be disturbed when he was working on his car, and would get extremely cross if anyone entered '*his garage*'. *What did he do in there with that blasted old, rust bucket of his?* She thought angrily, whilst placing the cup down on a cluttered side table outside the adjoining garage door. She'd often say to him 'You spend more time in there with that archaic automobile than you do with me and the babies. It's just not right for a man to neglect his family like you do. You're staying in there longer and longer these days.' He'd just walk off in a huff without saying a word, before slamming the garage door closed behind him. It was always locked.

'Tea!' She chirped loudly, like she always did - arms folded tightly with a scowl. There was no reply as usual, which made her blood boil. Placing her ear to the door she could hear the unhealthy sound of the engine spluttering away. Frustrated, Maggie imagined him lying on his back, underneath the corroded chassis, face mopped with jet black motor oil, tinkering – always tinkering. 'Don't forget, we're visiting the graveyard today!' She announced loudly, trying in vain to compete with the racket of the infernal metal contraption within. Every Saturday they'd visit Daniel's little grave, which was situated under a large, oak tree. It was a geometric masterpiece of polished black and grey granite surrounded by colourful stone chips. Deeply etched letters with a golden inlay read,
'Daniel Newman ~Our Angel in Heaven~'

Maggie would always place a solitary white rose at the foot of the small gravestone then she'd say a prayer and shed a tear. Her four babies were always well behaved when they visited their brother. The cruel stares were terribly heart breaking as she'd push the large four seat buggy up the street but Maggie didn't care. *They're just jealous; yes that's it, jealous of my four beautiful angels.*

'Hey, did you hear me?!' She yelled loudly. *It feels like he's been in there for days.* She thought venomously before knocking loudly over and over. Maggie almost burst into tears as he'd never missed a single visit to the graveyard. She knew she was probably losing him though. The constant shouting, the insane anger when he lost his patience with her was becoming unbearable. Ten years of marriage down the pan. Perhaps it was the way she'd let herself go physically. The lack of affection and her absentmindedness she'd developed over the last few months. Maggie composed herself; she had to be strong for the sake of her babies. She returned over to the kitchen and pulled on the rubber gloves firmly, completely forgetting about their feeds.

A loud knock on the front door barely registered with her ears. A second wrap caused her eyes to shift momentarily over to one side before returning their piercing stare outside once more. The frantic noise continued over and over again, and the sound of footsteps on the concrete driveway and flashing blue lights outside gave her no cause for concern. Relentlessly, she continued to scrub at the crockery, the clean crockery, with a worn out green scouring pad. The garden outside seemed to grow distant as though disappearing into another realm. A grey sky loomed overhead as a storm moved in. The high pitch splintering crack of the wooden door frame didn't sway her obsessive cleaning routine. The front door broke open and footsteps clattered on the wooden parquet flooring of the hallway towards her. A voice yelled out but to Maggie it sounded muffled as though screamed from inside another room. It shouted again then a powerful hand grasped her right shoulder. Her head began wobbling from side to side as she was shaken firmly. Her garden became an abstract vision of multi-coloured khaki foliage interspersed with the gloomy, Payne's grey sky. The smell of pollution was getting stronger, causing the group of people to cup their hands over their mouths. Maggie was completely oblivious.

'Mrs Newman, Mrs Newman!' said an authoritative male voice. There was no response. The desperate voice of her neighbour cut in.

'Maggie, it's Joan – my god something…' She was interrupted abruptly by the man.

'Not now Mrs Jameson, this is a police matter, now please don't interfere.' Mrs Jameson stared daggers at the policeman, biting the inside of her bottom lip until it bled profusely. He shook Maggie firmly again, suddenly tearing her from the deep trance. She turned swiftly and their eyes widened as she was brandishing a twelve inch carving knife. Bright light from the fluorescent above danced playfully along its razor sharp blade. Her wrist was automatically swinging the knife from side to side causing soap suds to drip from the pointed end down onto the floor tiles as she spoke.

'Why are you all here?'

'Maggie, please put the knife down, I'm Sergeant Harrison and I have something very important to…' He paused, his eyes opened wide as the knife was raised. Piercing shards of light flashed across his pale face. His fingers twitched and he was about to react when Maggie reached over and placed it gingerly onto the drainage rack. She looked about the kitchen almost oblivious to the small group of people who were now surrounding her.

'Well, what appears to be the problem officer?'

Her stinging eyes focused and just about recognised her friend. 'Joan, is that you? It's so good to see you. However, I do have lots to do today, and I need to...' She paused to think. 'Oh dear, I've completely forgotten. Oh well I'm sure I'll remember?' Joan burst into tears. The policeman straightened up as though preparing for a grand speech. His tone was melancholy as he spoke.

'Please Mrs Newman this concerns your husband Arthur, he's.'

'He's in serious trouble that's what he's in! Can't get him out of that damn garage and we've so much to do and so little time.' Suddenly, her nostrils flared as the suffocating pollution began to register. Her bright, green eyes seemed to blacken as though in shadow. 'What's that awful smell? I'll bloody kill him if he's come back in and forgotten to close the door behind him!' She headed off towards the connecting garage doorway. Her eyes shifted downward as thick, grey smoke bellowed from the slit at the bottom of it. The people followed her and were astonished as they saw countless mugs of stone cold tea stacked precariously on the side table, like some modern piece of sculpture. She didn't see the cups. She didn't see anything.

'If I've told him once, I must have told him a thousand times to place a damp towel at the foot of the door to keep the pollution out. It's not good for the babies breathing you understand?'

They just stared at her in disbelief, continuing to shield their mouths. The sound of the engine died. 'Finally, he's finished!' There was a sharp click from the other side of the door as it was unlocked. The handle turned and it was opened. Within the choking mist appeared a pair of uniformed figures. The large, metal, garage door had been slid open and rays of ghostly sunlight pierced inside the foreboding smog. The flashing blue light outside enveloped everything like a whirling disco ball. She looked at them with a look of confusion.

'Where's...?' They didn't react. Sergeant Harrison spoke softly.

'Mrs Newman, I'm very sorry to inform you that your husband has been found dead right here in your garage. According to the coroner he's been dead for hours. We'd like to ask you some questions at a more opportune time of course.' Joan was crying profusely now whilst edging closer towards Maggie.

'I'm so sorry.' She tried to embrace Maggie but was shunted away by her as though she were a stranger.

'Nonsense, he's...?' She stopped immediately, catching sight of something bright yellow which became clearer as the fog began to disperse. It was snaking its way from the exhaust pipe, right up inside the passenger window. *A death pipe.* She turned away not wanting to believe what she was seeing, then screamed out hysterically with her hands firmly over her face. Her teary eyes shifted from left to right, she thought she'd heard screaming from the baby monitor again.

Barging through the group of people, she headed off upstairs. She made her way into the nursery, tears streaming down her cheeks. The babies were sleeping soundly inside the darkened room. Relieved, she sat down in the corner, on a brightly coloured, stencilled, rocking chair which Arthur had painted many years ago. He'd been so good at things like that. Maggie began to sing a lullaby in the dusty shadows, rocking to and fro. Footsteps followed her upstairs and into the small nursery. The light was switched on and a look of bewildered astonishment was imprinted on their ruddy faces, as they saw them. They didn't want to see but there they were, all together.

Four cots, four blankets, four plastic dolls and Maggie with advanced dementia.

SECOND IN THE QUEUE

by

Simon Van der Velde

I follow the sound of semi-automatic fire up the staircase, and ease back the bedroom door. A man screams. Blood sprays from his severed thigh, and my fourteen-year-old son grunts in satisfaction. I lean in to kiss him goodbye. Eyes fixed on his alarmingly realistic PlayStation Six, he turns his shoulder and another victim howls in agony.

'I'm taking Sophie to dance, Charlie.' I tell him. 'Please don't trash the house.'

'Die,' he says, 'you bastards,' and another burst of gunfire follows me back down the stairs.

Sophie at least is still young enough to be interested in her dad. She takes my hand and skips beside me, practising some complicated dance step all along the pot-holed lane. She's still dancing when we pass the cricket ground and I remind myself how lucky we are to live in such a place, but the comforting sight of the pavilion is spoiled by the ragged row of identical posters glued to its wooden slats.

A masked man stands in the foreground with one fist raised to the sky, and the other pointing at me, while behind him a ball of flame bursts through a pretty, whitewashed house.

'Urban Justice', the caption reads, 'What they deserve'.

My hand tightens around Sophie's and I quicken my pace, away from the pavilion and up onto the broad sweep of Carlton Road.

'Don't want to be late,' I mumble, and squint against the glare from the gigantic new electro-board that hangs down beneath the railway bridge.

'Upgrade to Gold Star Care', it commands, while a thousand stars flash across the screen.

There's a four way junction on the brow of the hill, and the pedestrian crossing that cost a thousand signatures, back in the days when petitions still mattered. Sophie presses the button like she has since she had to stand on tip-toes to reach, and up close I see that the electro-board's alloy frame is pasted with a dozen more Urban Justice posters.

What fuels such rage, I wonder, as if the answer isn't right there in front of me, and I stare at my trainers and press down on my simmering guilt. I cannot be to blame. I have done nothing.

'Hey look,' Sophie says.

I feel an urge to cover her eyes, but Sophie isn't pointing at Urban Justice, she's staring wide-eyed at the giant billboard above us.

The stars have gone out, and a glossy teenage girl fills the screen.

'Red Surf Super Sale, still on,' Sophie reads, and I don't know whether to be pleased or appalled by my daughter's ability to filter the world around her.

'Yeh, right,' I say, relieved to fall back into that comfortable argument, 'a ten quid sweatshirt for only two hundred pounds.'

'Ten quid?' Sophie says, pointing alternate toes at the sloping curb. 'No one gets a top for ten pounds.'

'I do.'

That was a mistake.

'Yeh, Dad,' Sophie shakes her head at my 2016 Olympics t-shirt, so worn it's almost transparent. 'And it shows. I mean just look at the state…' and I'm pleased when her words are drowned by the roar of a big white Jaguar revving its engine at the lights.

'I'm just fine,' I tell her, but I can't help noticing that the neon chevron on the Jaguar's bonnet is flashing, meaning the on-board computer has been switched off and the driver is operating on manual override.

'That's not even legal anymore, not this close to town.'

Sophie shrugs.

The Jaguar growls.

I catch a glimpse through the windscreen. Black eye make-up and big hair. Rich kids in Daddy's car.

'Look the part, or be apart,' Sophie reads the Red Surf tag-line and looks up at me with that same ironic smile her mother used to have, before she took it to someone who could give her all the shiny things she wanted.

'Oh, belt up, Sophie. There are more important things than bloody money.'

She stops dancing. Her hand pulls out of mine.

I feel my jaw clench, unsure if I'm angry with Sophie or myself.

'Come on, Soph,' I say. 'Let's not spoil the day.'

Sophie's lips tighten. She stands, splay footed and angry at the edge of the curb.

I glare at the electro-board and wait for the green man to set us free. The little bugger stays stubbornly red, but the traffic light switches to amber.

The Jaguar surges forward. Fat tyres squeal. The car slips left, towards us. There's a gust of air. A momentary pressure.

I clutch the space where Sophie's hand should be, and take half a step back.

The steering wheel spins. Brakes bite. The nose dips, and that flashing chevron veers away. In the end, the back wheel barely clips the curb.

I see the girl in the passenger seat, the dragon tattoo on her arm, and the diamond at her throat. Her mouth opens. Blood sprays across the window. The car roars over the hill, and my hand is numb and empty.

Sophie lies at the edge of the curb. It must be her. She's wearing those sandals she made me buy, strappy, fussy things, white jeans, and a baby pink sweatshirt.

Her face is gone, lost behind a tangle of matted hair. Blood soaks down through her pink shirt, and I howl to match the roar of the engine.

I reach out, and draw away. I am terrified. That same fear as when I first saw her, pulled, bloody and screaming from her mother's belly. But now she is silent. The screams are mine.

'Sophie?'

I force myself to touch her, confused by the sticky heat on my fingers. Blood smears her face, like chocolate from some illicit treat. I kiss her and hold my ear to her lips, but all I hear is the click, click, click of mobile phone cameras from the gathering crowd.

Phone.

The thing slips in my hand. The screen will not recognize my bloody fingertips, but the God I no longer believe in smiles down upon me.

The lights change again and an ambulance edges forward. I stumble into the road, hands raised, blood running down my arms. The ambulance stops. The door opens. I look at the lines on the driver's face and try not to see the flashing gold star logo on the open door. But like Urban Justice, the logo is everywhere, on the bonnet of the ambulance, on his cap and trousers, and emblazoned across his chest, with his name, 'Ben', three black letters stark against the star.

'My daughter,' I begin, but there is nothing to say. She lies on the curb, with the crowd pressing in around her.

Ben puts his hand on my arm. He says something I do not hear, but his voice is calm, his grip warm and strong.

'Thank you,' I say, 'thank you, thank you,' and I sink to my knees on the road.

'Step away,' Ben commands. 'Don't move her, don't touch her.' He kneels by my daughter's side and cradles her head with gentle, knowing hands.

At the edge of my vision, the passenger door opens. A young woman steps down with her hair drawn back from her narrow forehead, and her name across the star on her buttoned-up blazer.

Courtney stands above me. Her palm opens and her mouth moves, but all I hear is the snapping of the crowd and the ringing in my ears.

'Thank you, thank you,' I say, as if they are the only words I know, but there is something in the tightness of Courtney's face that stills my tongue.

'I.D.,' she shouts over the clicking phones. 'I need to see your insurance.'

Her hand stretches and I stare at her long, thin fingers.

'Insurance,' she says again.

I fumble for my wallet and hold out my Silver Star NHS card, as if the watery sun might turn that base thing into gold.

Courtney's face sharpens. She jabs at the gold star on her chest.

'Come on, Ben,' she snaps.

He looks up, and I see that he has laid my daughter in the recovery position.

'She is alive,' I hear my own creaking voice.

Ben walks towards the ambulance.

'She needs help.' I grab his shoulder. 'For God's sake. Can't you see that?'

That's it,' Courtney says. 'Let's go.'

Ben lifts my hand from his shoulder. He, at least, has the decency to look ashamed.

'Wait.' I reach out, and then I think better of it. 'I have money.'

Courtney sneers at my worn out t-shirt and saggy joggers.

'There's a ten thousand deposit,' she says. 'More if she needs an operation.'

'Fine.'

She turns back to the ambulance.

'No. Please.'

'It's alright,' Ben says, and it is his turn to put a hand on my shoulder.

Courtney's back a moment later, with yellow plastic jutting from her pocket, and a mobile credit card machine. I hesitate, unsure what possible connection there can be between an ambulance and that machine. Ben nods encouragement. I push my card in and tap out the number with twenty years of regular payments behind me, not one of them anywhere near ten thousand pounds.

The technology is state-of-the-art. The answer is instantaneous.

Transaction declined.

I look from the grey screen to Courtney's arched eyebrows, and the urge to smash my fist into her brittle face is almost overwhelming.

'It's a mistake. An irregular transaction,' I garble the sort of jargon that Courtney might understand. And who knows, maybe it's true. I slap my pockets, and then see my phone lying on the road.

'Wait,' I tell her, 'just a moment,' and bang in the number on the back of the credit card.

God bless them. They answer on the first ring.

'I need an extension on my…'

'Thank you for calling Sky Blue Credit Cards. We are currently experiencing high volumes of calls. Your call is important to us and will be answered as soon as an operative becomes available. Please hold the line.'

My nails dig into my palms.

Sophie's blood drips onto the tarmac.

The phone beeps. A different voice comes on the line.

Hope surges hot through my chest.

'You are currently...*third*...in the queue.'

My breath catches in my throat and It Must Be Love comes screeching out of the phone, complete with trumpets and trombones.

'Ben. Help her, please.'

Ben steps from one foot to the other.

'Jesus Christ. It's only a mile to the hospital.'

Courtney says something about protocols.

'I'm sorry,' Ben turns back to the ambulance.

'No.' I spin him round and a flare goes up behind Courtney's eyes.

She grabs the yellow plastic from her pocket and holds it, two handed, at my throat.

'Tazers may be used in self-defence,' she says, like she's reading from a manual, like the voice on the end of the phone.

'You twisted cyborg. I'm going to ram that tazer...'

There's a noise behind me, a groan or a cry.

The snapping circle has closed around Sophie. I lash out, fighting my way through.

'Dad, Daddy,' she says, and a bubble bursts in her mouth.

I hold her hand. Now, when it's too late, I squeeze her palm tight against mine and look into her wide, bewildered eyes.

My vision blurs. I press her close. My baby's blood gushes onto my neck, while somewhere far away, an ambulance guns into life. Stars flicker and die on the board above us. 'What they deserve,' the poster screams. Finally, the sound of Madness stops beating through the phone, and we are second in the queue.

HIS MASTER'S VOICE
by
Jennifer Rowe

The robot hound waited patiently for its master to return.

When he did not, it lay down and rested its nose on its front paws, still, but alert to any sounds or unfamiliar smells in the air. The sky, once blue, was an angry orange and a wind from the North was beginning to ruffle the dog's fake fur.

Minutes turned into hours but it waited still, eyes turned toward the last sign of the man. When the number of days and nights ran into weeks and the sky had broken apart, turning the horizon into a swirling dark fire, and he had *still* not returned, it set its main life support systems to sleep, buried its muzzle a little into the remaining brown grass, and left only its basic programmes running.

Had a passing traveller glanced at the ground then, they would have seen nothing out of the ordinary - just a Border Collie crouched in the dirt. But there were no passing travellers now, nor would there be. It had been years since anyone had come this way. No real dogs with robot masters, no robot dogs with real masters, no salesmen in their Holo-cars , no Coptors crammed with tourists, even the Army-Stealthers had rounded up the final few and left. Nothing wished to live here anymore; little could. What was left of the human race was either being dispatched to waiting cargo-ships, impatiently orbiting the planet, or were already in the Sceptre galaxy where small settlements were earnestly developing new ways of living.

And yet there *had* been a master. The dog's simple circuits knew that. A man had stroked its fur-covered body, held its smooth head and looked into its camera eyes. There had been a master for 9,183 days. It had walked many miles with him, they had run together, it had fetched sticks and balls for him, it had lain at his feet in the Facility while the master had looked through a vast tube into the sky. They had stood together in the cool Algonquin forest and peered upwards at a star-smothered sky, they had roamed through that same forest, years later, as the trees dried to skeletons and the stars faded away.

'Stay, Larry. You stay here, OK?'

The Master had used his warm-voice, but the dog had sensed cold; two messages in one. It wagged its tail and took a tentative step forward.

'No, Larry'. The master had pointed to the floor. 'You stay now. You're all we've got left. I have to go.'

The dog wagged its tail once more, sat in the drying grass and watched its master walk away – first half as big, then half again and then when he was nearly nothing more than a speck, the ground below the giant dish seemed to open up and swallow him whole. Even then, the dog resisted the urge to follow, it resisted the urge to bound after him like it had done that morning and countless others, programmed to come to heel, to be a companion, to protect. It was programmed to be a dog, an obedient dog, a loyal friend; so he waited, just like he'd been told.

'It's coming, Larry. I have to go to the others. If they're still here, I have to, Larry, it's time.'

The man had bent low, stroked the dog's head, cupped its small skull and clicked something in place behind its jaw. He had looked into its eyes and then leaned forward, pressing his head into the synthetic fur of its neck. He let out a sound the robot dog did not understand. They stayed like that a while, the man's shoulders shaking and his unsteady breath heating the dog's coat. When he stood, his face was pink and the dog tasted salt in the air.

'You'll be fine, boy. You'll be fine. Just... stay.' That's when he had turned and walked away, and once he had been eaten by the distant earth, then nothing happened for a very long time.

*****

While the dog slept, the sky lit up like daylight once more, then darkened; the wind came and with it the dust-rain and fire-storms that washed its pelt almost free. Patches of fur and silicon skin clung around its haunches and stump of a tail, the metal below had weathered and lost its shine but beneath, a tiny hot furnace still glowed, repeating its message over and over.

'Wait, Larry, you have to wait.'

A long night fell, a night like no night before. Even small lichen and moss that had survived thus far slowly joined their neighbours in the dust. The dog waited, the dog slept.

Days, weeks, years passed – each time the sand and ash became too thick upon the dog's body, a tremor from within would shake it to the floor. Before it, and behind, lay nothing now but dunes and distance and far faint rumbles from the sky.

Still longer, and the dark clouds of the interminable night began to clear, first slowly, hinting that the sun still lived above and then, as the sky became a brown haze, sometimes a little water fell. And before long, more water and the dust drank in long gasps until microscopic plants hidden, dry and deep, like long forgotten secrets, began once more to search for the sun.

A long way off, a single light appeared in the Eastern sky, lighting the umber-washed nothing with a beam of white gold. It grew in size, and the air began to fizz with an unfamiliar energy. Something clicked in the dog's head. The furnace glowed brighter, sending electric synapses out across its resting circuits. With great difficulty, it sat up; the dust of the dead still caked its body so, to an unfocussed eye, a snow dog grew out of the earth. Its ears swivelled open. It howled, and howled again and again, the only sound in the wilderness.

The light grew bigger, brighter, formed two lights and, with it, a low buzz.

The dog howled.

The thing grew louder and bigger until the jets that powered its landing blew the dust around and around the dog. Its shadow encompassed it and landed no more than a few metres away. For a moment, nothing happened, nothing moved. Then, a hatch opened in the side of the vehicle, bright light shining from within. The dog tensed, its ears raised.

Two dark shapes stepped out onto the ash-snow soil. Their boots sank into the grey.

'Earth.' They said it together, with reverence. 'Earth.'

The dog's tail began to beat the hollow ground.

Their attention turned to the movement.

'Beacon located. Scan correctly identified.'

'A dog?', one whistled. She waved a metal stick in a circle around them and inspected it. 'Air's fine, helmets off.'

Together, they peered at the dog. One glanced at the other. 'Safe…?' The other nodded and they began walking towards it.

The dog whined and trembled in anticipation and then, as if readying itself to howl once more, it lifted its head and, from the depths of the tiny furnace, came its master's voice:

'Report 419, May 24, 2334.' The voice drifted loud and clear above the faint whirr of the cooling vehicle. 'Dr Andrew Wright of Standard Defence Division B: a summary of our last days before close contact. Asteroid is expected to enter the atmosphere within the next 24-48 hours. I've stayed up-side as long as I can but it's too late.' He laughed – a dry, unhappy sound. 'It was too late way before *this*. We expect surface disturbances here to be strong, estimate is minimal life for 30 years but the instruments are old so this is an approximation. We are the last four, I think. Forster, Ives and Kadinska are dead. We haven't heard from the other centres for more than eight months. The others are waiting for me in the survival tank and I'll continue audio reports from there. I've stayed above in the hope of finding another solution but let's face it, this rock's just the full stop at the end of a very depressing sentence. Our safest bet now is to get below ground until the Impact Winter ends.' A pause. 'I know we're only putting off the inevitable, but I can't stay up here any longer and watch the rest of it die. Larry – I mean, the beacon – has all our files and he'll monitor outcomes. He's built to withstand a lot but there's copies with us too. Uh, look, whoever finds this, I guess you're probably not going to hang around for long. When you go, don't – don't leave him, the dog I mean, don't leave him here when you go. Christ, this is going to sound stupid. He doesn't like being alone. He's more than just... he's my dog.'

His voice softened. 'Hey, Larry, good job, my friend, good dog.'

The new astronauts looked at one another. One held her hand towards the dog. 'Um. Larry?'

As quick as a rocket the dog shot towards the astronauts, sniffing, whining, trembling with anticipation. If they had not recognised it as a dog before, they would have been sure at this. But although the dog's sensors were now functioning normally, it could not find the smell that went with that voice – the voice that said 'good dog'. Without warning, it stiffened and galloped away, past the crew in their radiation suits and across the sands. It stopped abruptly half a mile or so away, scrabbling at the sand.

When they caught up with it, they found the facility, and beneath that the hatch, the mummified bodies and the equipment that had failed to save their world. While they finalised their search, the dog slumped beside the corpse of Dr Wright, and though it was easily called away, trotting along obediently beside the two astronauts, they noticed that it often looked back.

As they sat at the controls, readying the ship for its return journey to the 58th Planet, the dog curled like any other real dog in one of the passenger seats.

The older woman sucked her teeth. 'Thirty years! Boy, they had no idea, did they?'

'That old hound's better at being alone than anyone else I've ever met,' chuckled her second-in-command. And they set their coordinates for home – the home where they were born, where their parents were born, and their grandparents and great-grandparents before them.

GIRL POWER

by

Barbara Young

Gloston Daily Post

Missing Girl

Fifteen-year-old schoolgirl Gina Watson has been missing for two weeks. Last seen on Sunday, July 17, Gina left home to meet some friends in a local park, but she did not arrive. Police have mounted a full-scale operation: searching nearby houses and woodland, interviewing hundreds of people, and, later today, will conduct a reconstruction of Gina's supposed route on the day she disappeared. Gina is the fourth local girl to go missing in the last twelve months...

Okay, I'm in. I feel slightly disorientated, but I know they're at home – I can hear voices and a television blaring.

The hallway is narrow and dark, its wooden floorboards partially covered by a thin rug splashed with toxic-looking stains. The air is thick and sour, making me lightheaded. Maybe my breathing is off.

I look down the hallway at a small door on the left-hand side, under the stairs. That's where I should go, but just seeing it turns the air to treacle. I tentatively approach the room they're sitting in and peer inside.

She's sprawled on a grungy, cream-coloured sofa, which is angled slightly away from me. Her huge thighs bulge in tight black leggings. She crams a biscuit into her mouth, her attention focused on the TV screen. A newsreader is announcing the imminent reconstruction of a missing girl's last known movements.

"They'll be coming right past our front door," she says, laughing through a harsh cough, biscuit crumbs spraying onto the floor.

"Well, you can always invite them in for tea, give them the guided tour, show them our collections," he says, taking a long drag on his cigarette. One skinny hand ferrets under his belt and rubs vigorously at his groin.

Anger spikes through me. How can they laugh and eat and scratch, knowing what they know, doing what they do? Fear washes through my anger but I shake it off. I've got a purpose, though I'm not sure how to achieve it. I breathe deep, focus on the anger, let it grow. I need it.

I creep silently from the room and down the hallway, towards the dull green door under the stairs. The paint is flaking, battered by time. The bolts at the top and bottom look flimsy, but there is a heavy lock near the handle – no key. I made it through the front door, so this should be a doddle. I can hear their voices in the background: he is shouting something about the police. My head is thumping and I know I haven't got much time. I've got to get this done.

I launch myself and I'm through. Standing at the top of a flight of stairs. They are steep and narrow and it's dark down there. There's a smell – mould and something worse: something rotten. It's cold and I can feel my skin tingling. I stand absolutely still, listening. I don't want any surprises. There is silence. Then, behind the silence, there is scurrying, scrabbling; small creatures rustle in corners. I hear the wisp of a breath beneath me.

Despite the dark I can see okay. Shapes are emerging in the cellar: boxes piled high against one wall, a pair of step-ladders lying amongst a tangle of paint pots, an old bicycle tilted upside down in a corner.

I edge my way down the stairs and, finally, I see the bed tucked in the alcove beneath the stairs, where it's always been. Down here, the smell is worse. A girl is lying on a filthy, grey mattress that is smeared with dark stains.

She is curled up on her side, knees tucked beneath her chin. Dressed only in a tattered red dress. Her dark hair is long and matted around her face. Her body is tethered by a chain around her neck to an iron ring on the floor, and she is covered in bruises; some old and faded, some livid with fresh pain.

"Gina." I whisper her name and lean close. There is no reaction: she is totally out of it. I grasp her shoulder and shake it, my face inches from hers – I can smell her fetid breath.

"Gina." I am shouting now, oblivious to the danger of them hearing me.

"*Gina*," I scream into her face. She doesn't move. I can see she is breathing; her chest is rising and falling. I try to get my hands under the iron bracelet around her neck, but it is too tight. The chain linking it to the floor rattles against the metal ring on the ground. Her head whips around at the sound and she stares straight through me.

"*Gina*," I scream again, frustration burning a hole in my gut, drowning me.

"You're wasting your time. She can't hear you." The voice startles me. I flinch, turning slowly towards the sound. I thought we were alone in the cellar.

I make out a dim figure in the corner, a girl about my own age, with short blonde hair, pale skin and a sarcastic twitch to her lips. Her grubby – once white – sundress hangs off her thin frame. She looks like a prom queen with a serious case of anorexia.

"What the…?" My voice is barely a whisper; my vision blurs. I step away from Gina.

"Very admirable, Zoey," the girl says. "But you don't stand a hope in hell of getting her free from that necklace. You need reinforcements." She moves closer, and I can see her white skin is mottled with purple blotches.

I am not afraid of this girl. She is going to help me, although I don't know how.

Gina is twisting her head from side to side. She can't see us as we are both standing behind her, but she knows we are here.

The girl beckons me away from the bed and perches on the bottom step. Somehow, I know her name is Kelly.

"We haven't got much time. Ten minutes tops and the reconstruction will be outside. That's when we do it." She grins like a bloody Cheshire cat, and I feel a spike of irritation – I can't see what's to grin about.

"What exactly do you have in mind?" Another girl appears out of the gloom, dressed in a blue school uniform – she is even more dishevelled, with messy red curls framing a face full of freckles. Her green eyes burn with anger. The same twitch to her lips as Kelly.

"Hey, Susie," says Kelly. "Welcome to the party, if a little late. You're looking a tad worn at the edges, if you don't mind me saying."

"Right back at you; you're doing such a good impression of Jennifer Lawrence. Not."

I should be confused by all this, but I'm not; on some level that I can barely grasp, it makes perfect sense. I glance back towards Gina; she is twisting on the bed, trying to see behind her. Eyes wide.

"Where are you?" Gina asks, her voice low, almost a whisper.

Susie is at her side in a heartbeat. She strokes Gina's matted hair and traces a finger down her cheek.

"Oh babe, it's okay. It's going to be okay. I promise, we're going to get you out of here."

Gina doesn't reply, but her body calms.

"Right, we've only got a few minutes to get this together. It has to be timed just right." Kelly turns towards me, lays a hand on my arm. Her touch is feather-light; I can barely feel it.

"Susie and me are going to do our thing upstairs," she says. "Zoey, you stay down here with Gina and concentrate on the door." She tilts her chin up the stairs to the only exit.

My blurred vision is getting worse; pain grips my head like a vice. Kelly seems to fade for a moment, her thin body almost transparent. I shake my head, clearing the fog. I need to find some strength.

"A little explanation would be helpful, I'm not a mind reader," I say. My voice surprises me with its force as my eyes flick between the two girls.

Susie steps forward, takes me by the arm and we sit on the bed, side by side. Gina ignores us, staring at the ceiling.

"Kelly, ease up a bit. Zoey needs to understand before we can do this." Susie smiles reassurance at me and I nod in agreement. My gaze switches to Kelly who is tapping her foot impatiently, arms firmly crossed in front of her.

"Seriously! Bloody rookies." Kelly huffs out a breath. "Okay. Here it is – the plan. We are going to create such a shit-storm in this house when the reconstruction comes past that the police are going to charge in; Gina will be found and we will be total heroes. Simple." She laughs, a brittle fragile sound, not a lot of mirth there. "Then maybe we can all get some bloody sleep."

I shake my head in frustration. Susie and Kelly don't look strong enough to swing a cat. Gina is chained to the floor and I'm feeling seriously blurred around the edges.

"And just how are we going to do that?" I ask. It is my foot that is tapping now.

Kelly grins at Susie. "The girl sure is slow on the uptake," she drawls in an American accent. "You explain." Her hand draws an invitation from Susie to me.

Susie turns to me. "Okay. Basic facts. You know you're not…as you were?"

I glance down at my body; it flickers back at me. Of course I know, even if I don't want to admit it.

"But, we do have something going for us," Susie says, a grin splitting her face into something wonderful. "Think about it. What have we got in common? What does it mean?"

"We're teenage girls," Kelly chips in.

"We're angry."

"Possible mental health issues."

"Speak for yourself." Susie does an eye roll.

"We are seriously pissed off teenagers," she continues. "We do not deserve what has happened to us but we are going to save this girl.

"Come on, Zoey, you've seen the films. Think *Carrie,* well, not exactly, something more recent, a remake of an old classic – starts with a P... o... l... t... e... r...g..." Her finger ticks off each letter as she says it. "I'm talking really scary stuff, teenage heaven, we all loved it." She pauses for a moment. "So, what do we do best?"

Realisation dawns in a warm rush. Now it's me doing the Cheshire cat grin. Finally, I get it.

"We throw things."

Gloston Daily Post

Dramatic Rescue

The search for missing teenager Gina Watson came to a dramatic conclusion last night. A reconstruction of the girl's last known movements was interrupted by a loud disturbance at 38 Main Street. She was found in the basement of the property and two people are in police custody.

A neighbour told us that she often heard the owners of the property arguing; but this was far worse than usual. "It was like all hell was let loose – there was shouting and screaming, thuds and bangs, then a television was thrown through the window. I've never heard anything like it."

The police entered the house, and sometime later, John and Mary Dodds were led into a police car. The witness said they were both shaking and looked "as white as ghosts".

Gina is in hospital, and is said to be doing well. Her injuries are not thought to be life-threatening.

A police source informed us that three bodies had been found buried in the back garden. They have not yet been formally identified but are believed to be the missing girls: Susie West; Kelly Brown; and Zoey Burns.

LEAD TEARS
by
Anne Walsh Donnelly

I draw another tear with my pencil. The lead scrapes against the wall as I colour it in. I'm afraid Nanny will get to see all the tears if she starts cleaning in here but I don't want to rub them out. She's upstairs in my bedroom now, her hoover is giving me a headache as it sucks the life out of the carpet. My heart batters the walls of my ribcage. This must have been how children in the war felt hiding in their basements waiting for the bombs to drop.

"I'm cleaning out the storeroom today," Nanny said to me over breakfast. "It's time to get rid of the rubbish in there."

"That's my cubbyhole," I said, dropping my spoon into my bowl.

"You're getting too old for a cubbyhole."

I wanted to shout. No. But she was using her don't-argue-with-me voice so I kept the "No" in my mouth along with the cornflakes that had stuck to the roof of it.

I kept the words in the day she told me about Mam.

"She took a heart attack and died."

I closed my eyes real tight and put my hands over my ears. How do you *take* a heart attack? It's not as if you can go into Dunnes, see it on a shelf beside the bread and say to yourself - I'm fed up of living, I'll take that.

If Nanny thinks I'm letting her into my cubbyhole she's got another thing coming. There's no rubbish in here that needs clearing out. What would I sit on if she threw out the boxes? And they're full of Mam's dresses, shoes and handbags. I close my eyes, lean back against Mam's fur coat that hangs from a hook on the wall behind me, pull it around my face and breathe in her smell as the fur tickles my nose. It's not as sweet as the perfume Nanny uses. She calls Mam's smell, mildew. I don't care what it's called. This is mine and Mam's place. She can't take that away from me.

The key screeches as I turn it in the lock. I'm safe now. I couldn't believe my luck this morning when I found it in one of the kitchen drawers while Nanny was hanging out the washing.

I can hear the hoover plug being pulled from the socket in my bedroom. Then thump, thump, thump as Nanny drags it down the stairs.

"Once I've the bathroom cleaned you'll have to come out of there," she says, as she passes on her way to the kitchen.

I pull Mam's coat even tighter until I hear Nanny's feet on the bathroom tiles. Then I open the coat and look at the photo of Mam that I blu-taked to the ceiling. It's amazing how you can see through the dark if you stare hard enough.

I talk to her sometimes but I never hear her voice. I'm going to make a Mother's Day card today so we can put it on her grave when Dad comes home from the Lebanon.

"Your father won't be too happy if you're still in there when he arrives home this evening," shouts Nanny from the bathroom.

Now there's something stinging the inside of my nose and it's in my eyes too. Nanny's gone green so she's using vinegar for cleaning. It's cheaper too, she says. But the smell of it is ten times worse than the smell of Flash or Domestos.

The bathroom window creaks as she opens it. Thank God for that. The vinegar might go and sour someone else's house. Then there's a shuffle outside the cubbyhole. The handle squeaks as it's pushed down but the door doesn't budge. She lets out one of her big sighs. It seems to go on forever and I wait for her to breathe.

"Open the door. Please."

She sighs again.

"I'm going to make a cake. I could do with some help."

Her voice is softer now and it almost sounds as if she's going to cry. But Nanny doesn't do tears.

Though, I thought I saw a tear hanging out of one of her eyes last Saturday when she caught me wearing one of Mam's dresses. It was the one with lots of flowers all over it that she's wearing in the photo with Nanny on the mantelpiece in the sitting room. Nanny was laughing in the photo, so I thought if I wore it she might laugh again. I had closed my eyes after putting it on and it hugged me just like Mam does in my dreams. It felt soft and slinky on my skin and I wanted to keep it on forever.

But Nanny didn't laugh. She just scrunched up her face real tight and dragged her fingers across her forehead as if she was trying to iron out the creases.

She's tapping on the door now.

"You can lick the bowl and spoon if you want," she says.

I dig my teeth into the top of my pencil.

"Okay, suit yourself."

I hear her slippered feet move towards the kitchen.

I jiggle my legs to get rid of the pins and needles creeping into them. Stretch my arms as far as the ceiling will let me. It's stuffy in here so I turn the key ever so quietly and push the door open just enough to let a spurt of air and slice of light in. My eyes blink.

The eggs crack in the kitchen. Then, the whizz of the electric beater. There's the scraping of a spoon around the sides of the bowl and it makes my mouth water.

The oven sends out waves of cake smells. The sourness of the vinegar. Smothered in sweetness. I lean towards the crack in the door. Deep breath. Suck the cake smells in. I'm like one of those rats in the Pied Piper of Hamelin. But I can't leave or I might never get back in here again.

The clattering of dishes in the sink hurts my ears. Then the rustle of the newspaper that Nanny couldn't be reading 'cos she's turning the pages too fast. I should have brought "Lilly Alone" with me. But then how could I read it in the dark? I wonder what will happen next in the story. Lilly's parents are separated and she's never seen her dad. I turn her story over and over in my mind to try and forget about the cake in the oven.

"I'm taking it out," Nanny says, in a raised voice.

A whoosh of air escapes from the oven. Then an almighty clatter on the kitchen tiles. I jump and hit my head off the ceiling. It's throbbing and I feel a bump pushing through my scalp.

Someone makes funny breathing sounds. I push my cubbyhole door open a bit further and peek out. Nanny's body is shaking. She must be having another one of her little turns. I shove the door wide open and run to the kitchen. She's on the floor, surrounded by bits of sponge.

"Nanny!"

I trample over the cake bits and pull at her to get up. She's too heavy.

"I'm sorry," I cry. "It's all my fault."

She stops shaking.

"Nanny?"

The noise coming from her mouth frightens me. She pulls me to her and I think I'm going to suffocate.

"Don't die, Nanny, I couldn't bear it."

She hugs me even tighter and the two of us stay on the floor, taking breaths together. I feel her chest rise and fall. She's going to be okay, I think.

"Can you stand, Nanny?"

"In … a … minute."

When we finally get up, she sits on a chair and I get her a glass of water. She takes a sip. I search her face for some colour as I rub my hand across the top of her back.

"Are you ok, Nanny?"

"Tissue," she says, as she grabs my hand. It's so cold.

I let go, run and take a bunch from the box on the worktop and give them to her. She wipes her face, takes a huge breath and sighs, then another breath.

"I'm dying for a cup of tea," she says.

I make one that you could trot a mouse on, as she sometimes says, and put an extra spoonful of sugar in it, 'cos that's supposed to be good when you've had a shock. Then I get the brush and sweep up the bits of cake on the floor.

"Thanks, pet, you're a great help."

She looks much better now that she's finished the tea. I sneak a look out to the hall where my cubbyhole door blocks the light from the front door's frosted glass.

"I saw a lovely bean bag in Dunnes last week. It would be nicer than sitting on those hard boxes," she says.

"Can we get a pink one?"

"Absolutely and we could get a torch too. Then you could draw and read in your cubbyhole."

I could do with drawing some tears now, I think, as I look from Nanny to the hall and back again. Then something runs down my cheek.

"Don't throw my mam away."

"Nobody can do that," she says as she puts her hand over my chest. "Your mam's right here; in your heart."

She hands me one of the tissues and I wipe my eyes.

"Can we make another cake before we take out the boxes?"

"Of course, pet."

"And I want to keep Mam's fur coat and the purple flowery dress."

A mix of a laugh and a cry come out of Nanny's mouth.

Then the front door bursts open and someone tramps through the hall banging the cubbyhole door shut.

"Dad!"

He drops his bag on the floor and gives me a big hug. As I breathe in his army smells I hope he doesn't notice the sticky floor and the pile of tissues on the table. Nanny gets up and puts them in the bin.

"Is everything ok?" he asks her.

I can feel his hot breath on the top of my head.

"Just a bit tired. We've been very busy today and we were just about to make a cake to celebrate you coming home," she says.

I wonder if I should tell Dad about her little turns but he might put her into a home. Then who'd look after me? He might get another wife and I don't want a new mammy.

After dinner they go into the sitting room to watch the news. I sneak into my cubby hole but leave the door open so I can hear them talking.

"She's not still going into that pokey hole under the stairs, is she?"

"There's no harm in it and it's where she feels closest to her mam," says Nanny.

The man on the news starts to speak louder. I draw a picture on Mam's card with the crayons Dad brought me. When I'm finished I look up at her photo.

"Happy Mother's Day ... sometimes I wish you'd talk back to me."

I close my cubbyhole door to block out the noise from the telly and put my ear up to her photo but she still doesn't say anything so I snuggle into her fur coat. At least when I get my new beanbag, it will be much comfier in here and maybe when I get a bit older I'll be able to rub away the tears with my eraser.

TAKE THE GAMBLE
by
John Bunting

The first time Wendy caught sight of Zac, he was shaking his head sadly as she threw up over the daffodils in the Municipal Remembrance Gardens. She lunged at him unsteadily, determined to punch his sanctimonious face, but was stopped by a handcuff-wielding policeman. The first time Wendy spoke to Zac was four days later, outside the Magistrates' Court where she'd been fined £80 for being drunk and disorderly. It was to be a conversation that would test them both to the limit.

The dank, February mist hung heavy as Wendy marched angrily down the street, muttering vile curses on the Judge and his family. She felt a tap on her shoulder. "Excuse me," said a man's voice hesitantly, "can I speak to you?"

She swung round angrily. "Leave me alone, sodding press." Then she saw who it was. "Oh hell, not you again." She aimed her umbrella at his groin. "Buggar off!"

Zac swerved to avoid her death-thrust. "Steady! I want to help."

"That's what all you bastards say." Wendy wiggled her bottom at him insultingly. "Talk to the arse."

"I can think of better things to do with it."

Wendy squared up to him teapot fashion. "I might have bloody guessed. That'll cost you a hundred."

"Oh no, I don't... oh dear. I was just trying to get your attention. My name's Zac, and I've been sent to give you spiritual guidance."

"Who by? The bleeding Jehovahs?"

"Goodness me, no; dreadful people. I'm a sort of guardian angel."

"I knew it!" snorted Wendy. "You're a sodding nutter."

"No, I am... not a nutter... look, let me buy you a coffee, and I'll explain." Zac smiled. "I must say, you have got lovely ears."

"Jeez," spluttered Wendy, "arse *and* ears; you're a perv as well as a nutter." She turned to walk off, but Zac pushed round, blocking her path.

"Sorry," he groaned, "I'm not very good at this am I? One more chance... please!"

For the first time, Wendy looked at him properly. He was early-twenties, tall and fair with a kindly face. "All right, I suppose you are quite good looking. You can buy me a double vodka."

"Sorry again," shrugged Zac, "that's against the rules. How about a full English?"

Wendy's eyes lit up. "Now you're talking."

Ten minutes later they were sat in 'Rumbling Tums'. Wendy hadn't eaten all day, and pitched straight into her fry-up. She knew Zac was watching her, and could imagine what he was thinking – that she was probably about twenty-five, but the booze made her look a wan and puffy-faced fifty; that her tarty clothes were too tight, her hair too bleached, and her make-up too heavy. She wondered if he knew why. Only when she'd cleared her plate did she look up. "OK, pretty perv, talk."

Zac took a deep breath. "I've been sent to help you find a new path in life; a way out of your troubles. You'll be dead in five years if you carry on drinking like you are. You're my first assignment, by the way; I only completed my training a month ago."

There was a long pause. Then Wendy said, "Finished? Good. You are bleeding Jehovahs, aren't you?"

"No, I'm the real deal."

"The real deal what?"

"Guardian Angel."

"You're telling me you've been sent from… up there." Wendy shook her head dismissively. "That's bollocks."

"I can prove it." Zac leaned over, and whispered in her ear for several seconds.

Wendy sat back hard in her chair, and stared at him wide-eyed. "No! I never reali… Oh shit, that means… you know…"

"Indeed it does. And I'm impressed."

"By what? My arse? So you keep saying."

Zac laughed. "Touché. By your grasp of the implications."

"I used to be clever," said Wendy sadly. "I got a first at Oxford."

"You've fallen a long way since then."

"You're not kidding."

"Do you want to talk about it?"

Wendy made a big thing of not wanting to; taking off her coat, and hanging it slowly over the back of her chair. Then she sighed noisily. "You haven't got a ciggy have you?" Zac sat silent. "Of course not, you're a bloody Angel." She sighed again. "All right… there was this woman; she was a partner at the law firm I joined after Oxford. Before her, there had only been spotty boys and smelly students. She was beautiful, intelligent, forceful; everything I'd dreamt of being. I couldn't resist her advances; didn't want to. But she used and abused me, and then spat me out. I was destroyed. Shit, I still am." Wendy started to cry, tears dripping onto her empty plate.

Zac passed her his napkin. "You gave up the law?"

"I fell in with a card sharp. I was the distraction while he fixed the deck. We drank and cheated our way round the country for a couple of years. Then one day I woke up, and he'd gone."

"And since then?"

"There's been nothing since then. I spend my days playing the slot machines, and drinking bootleg vodka." Wendy blew her nose, and dabbed her eyes. "I can't face the world any more, it hurts too much."

"So you booze, and swear, and dress like a tart to push people away?"

"Jeez, you don't hold back, do you?" sobbed Wendy. "I guess so."

Wendy asked Zac to get her another coffee. She needed time to gather herself, and she could see that he needed a break too; that being face to face with this broken woman was hard for him. She smiled through her tears as he brought the coffee over. "I'm one hell of a first assignment, aren't I?"

"Drink it up," said Zac, "it's strong and hot." He laughed. "Hey, like me!"

Wendy took a sip. "You're sweet. Is the point where you have a word with Upstairs, and He makes everything better?"

"Sorry, that only happens in the movies. In reality, you have to sort things out for yourself."

"Do you think I haven't tried?"

"Have you spoken to anyone? Asked for their help?"

"The Court sent me for counseling, but I could tell they didn't care." Wendy shrugged. "Sod them, I stopped going."

"What about friends?"

"They disappeared fast."

"Family?"

"My parents have disowned me." Wendy looked down at her cup, and then added almost as an afterthought, "There's my sister; I haven't spoken to her for years. She's got everything; husband, kids, a good job. She knows what I've become, though, she wouldn't be interested."

"How do you know? Get in touch with her."

Wendy shook her head fiercely. "No. Leave my sister out of this. Drink is the only thing that can help me now."

"That's rubbish. In my experience talking to someone you trust is the best way."

"In your experience!" sneered Wendy. "What experience? You're a bloody trainee."

"Yes, damn it," snapped Zac, "my experience. I was a dropout junkie. My wife and kids walked out on me. I died a week later from a heroin overdose. A deliberate heroin overdose. Don't *ever* question my experience."

Wendy reached over. "Oh, I'm sorry, I didn't... sorry."

Zac pulled his hands away. "Yes, yes, me too; this is about you, not me."

For the next hour, Wendy talked about the hell she'd fallen into; the alcohol, the shop lifting, and the gambling. And sometimes, when she needed the money, the nameless men. Zac kept encouraging her to look on the positive side, to find ways she could help herself. But nothing he said could shake her belief that her life was ruined. Eventually, they fell silent, and sat staring uneasily at each other.

"So, my pretty Angel, what now?"

Zac shook his head. "I don't know. Tell me more about your sister. Were you close once?"

"When we were younger," Wendy said bitterly. "She's eighteen months the older; the sensible one. She was always there with a shoulder when I needed it. She got me out of a lot of hairy corners when we were teenagers. And what did I do in return? I went up to Oxford, and dropped her for the bright lights." Wendy wiped her nose. "I've never forgiven myself. I doubt she's forgiven me."

Zac's eyes flashed. "So I ask you again. Why don't you get in touch with her, and find out?"

"And I've told you to leave my sister out of this!"

"But why, Wendy, why?"

"Because... damn you... don't you see?" Wendy banged her fist on the table angrily. "I'm frightened she'll put the bloody phone down on me! I can't take that gamble."

Zac banged his fist down too, deliberately matching her anger. "Then don't phone her. Fix the deck. Go and see her unannounced; just walk in, and sit down."

"That's crazy. She'd throw me out."

"So she might, but there's a chance she might not. There's a chance she still has a shoulder for her little sister, and will want to help her out of another hairy corner. Remember how you loved her for that?"

"Wendy started to cry again, fear growing. "You bastard."

"But I could be right!" shouted Zac. "It might be your last chance. Take the gam—"

"Fuck you!" screamed Wendy, jumping up and slapping his face. "Don't you dare do this to me!"

Zac stood up too, and jabbed his finger at her. "I will dare, because I'm telling you the truth, and deep down you know it. You're just too frightened to risk it."

Wendy slapped his face again, harder. "Sod you, fucking Guardian fucking Angel. I wish I'd never met you. Now... now you've said these things... fuck you!" She grabbed her coat, and ran to the door. As she hauled it open, she heard Zac shout after her, "Take it, Wendy. Take the gamble!"

Wendy ran stumbling down the street, barging and cursing past the shoppers, until she reached the steps of the Methodist church. Looking round to make sure Zac hadn't followed, she went inside. She leaned against the wall at the back, and stared at the altar cross; letting her mind drift through what Zac had said to her. Above all, that fear he had forced her to confront. Was contacting her sister really her last chance? Dare she take that risk? What if—"

A gentle voice broke her thoughts. "How do you think he got on?"

Wendy looked up at the huge crucifix hanging over the altar. "Not bad. He found it hard, but that was to be expected. He asked the right questions, and he was tough when he had to be. He took a bit of gamble himself, though, trying to get me to face up to what might be my last chance. If I don't, well…"

"I'll have a word. You were very convincing, as usual. They never guess."

"Thank you. Was he a junkie?"

"Yes, a sad case. What's your next step?"

"I'll engineer an 'accidental' meet with him tomorrow, and eventually let him persuade me to go and see my 'sister'. He fancied me, you know."

"Bits of you, anyway," smiled the voice. "Could he cope with a real assignment?"

"As long as he or she isn't too pretty!"

"Good. Thank you, as ever. Your work testing out new Guardians is invaluable."

"When can I ascend again? These sessions are tough on me too."

"I know. Hopefully next month. There's someone else I'd like you to check out first. Up in Manchester; Theresa."

Wendy sighed. "Another? All right, if I must. But please not vodka this time, it makes me so sick."

The voice laughed. "I saw."

"Drugs, maybe. Coke is fun."

"Steady! I can't see the Heavenly Host agreeing to us getting married if you're a junkie!"

Wendy giggled, and wagged her finger at the crucifix. "Gotcha. Only kidding, I'll stick to the vodka." She turned to leave. "Let me know about Theresa."

"I will. I can't wait to start our new life together, Wendy. Love you."
"Love you."

HERE NOR THERE

by

Jeff Drummond

I lurk on the landing and peer over the banister. I feel the rush of a warm summer air enter the house through the open front door and watch as she flounces in.

My senses are displaced momentarily, the sound of her heels on the laminate floor and the vision of her navy-skirted suit undulate through my consciousness like waves stroking a beach, her jovial laugh and inconsequential prattle echo as a ball would rattle around in a pin-ball machine.

She has two people in tow, two more prospective buyers, and I wonder, not for the first time who will gain financially from the sale of my house.

The air settles and I see the young couple clearly. The girl is holding the man's hand and smiling. And he – he is taking in everything – his nose quivers like a rodent sensing the morning air. Most people did that on entering, and those who did rarely stayed long.

I enter the loft through the broken trap door; I do not want to be around when the couple are shown the bedrooms. Some detect my scent and turn their snouts to the heavens. They ask what it is. Flouncy-pants as usual recites the same answer – the house has been empty too long – it needs the windows open to let in the fresh air. 'Why is it so cheap?' they ask. 'The owner wants a quick sale,' is the reply. The owner – that's a laugh. I want to tell them I am the owner, but I can't.

A few people have asked for a peek in the loft, and the steps in the back bedroom make it easy for them. I wish the confounded things weren't there. All ask why there is no trap door. I could tell them, but again, I can't.

I listen from my hiding place behind the old water tank – a tank now empty since I had the combination boiler installed. I hear the steps being hauled into place and watch as heads stretch into the darkness like meerkats. But with no floorboards they never venture far inside. I imagine they are looking for any sign of light through the old slate roof. I would like them to explore further, but I want them to buy the house – not flee it like the crew of a sinking ship.

They leave, and once again the house and I are at one in solitude.

Time passes swiftly as I drift in and out of consciousness. I never go out – not any more. Sometimes I settle in the front bedroom and watch the world go by through a grubby bay window. I see neighbours washing their cars – children playing in the close. They never see me. I watch for hours – or is it days? I really don't know. Time is like the drifting sand on the surface of a vast desert, random and rebellious.

The key turns in the front door and once again I wait for flouncy-pant's spiel. But no heels perpetrate an attack on my weakening senses. Intrigued, I move out of the room and peer over the banister.

It's hard to describe the thrill I feel at seeing the last happy couple who viewed the house. I have no fluttering heart; no belly to fill with butterflies. But I do have an urge – an overpowering desire to have someone live with me, someone other than the deceitful whore I married. And I know if I do everything just right my wife will pay for what she did to me – and that scheming, back-stabbing mate of mine – he will get his comeuppance too. And to think he was my best man.

The couple are unescorted. The girl has a tape measure; the man strokes his chin thoughtfully.

"We could turn one of the bedrooms into a music room," I hear him say. His words come to my ears distantly dream-like. My hearing has never been good since the fall. Again I retreat to the attic. I don't want my presence felt – not yet.

Time flies in the blink of an imaginary eye. I remain in my spot behind the tank and hear the sound of work in the rooms below. The trap door has been fixed but it is not a problem, I can still get out.

Sometimes, I watch the new owners sleeping in the back bedroom. The man always becomes restless in my presence. His eyes twitch rapidly, and I can only wonder what effect I am having on his dreams.

All of my furniture and possessions are gone – all the things that the bitch left behind and did not want. Now the house doesn't feel like mine anymore. Now it belongs to Jamie and Emma.

The front bedroom where my treacherous wife and I made love is now Jamie's beloved music room, and I watch with interest as he builds and plays his acoustic guitars. His voice is evocative, reminding me of so many good years. His music would bring a tear to my eye – if I had one.

Emma is so pretty; she dances into the room like porcelain on air while he plays. She sings beautifully, and I watch the flame of love intertwine. But with it comes a pang of envy to my restless soul. They have what I should have had, but I bear no malice.

Sometimes he would stop working if I filled his space. I would see his nostrils flare and sniff the air – his face crinkling in repulsion. He would march out of the room and breathe in the air on the landing, then he would press his nose to the air vent set into the blocked up fireplace. But he would always return to stand in front of me – peering into my space.

Today, he spoke whilst taking delicate shavings off the stem of a new guitar. He stopped working and spun in his chair, eyes wide with puzzled trepidation.

"Hello again," he said.

I desperately want to say 'hello' back, but my existence is merely an echo of my former self.

I move away. He follows.

We are on the landing now – below the trap door. I effortlessly rise and watch him turn through three-sixty. His nostrils flutter like paper on a breeze. Slowly, he returns to the bedroom.

My descent is swift. He stops, turns, and once again he detects my presence.

"What are you?" I hear him say. Tramlines grace his forehead, a cropped head of short hair lies to one side.

A hand passes through me and I momentarily lose consciousness.

"Are you a ghost? Whatever you are you smell really bad."

Again he follows my stinking scent to the landing. I rise again – slowly this time. He lifts his head and I see his eyes narrow. The hairs on the back of his neck bristle.

He bolts for the stairs. I want to shout. I want to follow him but I can't go down to the ground floor. I have willed myself to do so on many an occasion but I never get any further than the half-landing. It is out of bounds. I don't know why.

I retreat to my water tank disgruntled and frustrated. I was so close that time. They would leave now. No one wants to live in a haunted house.

Time drifts, and light penetrates the darkness of my sanctuary – one beam of light followed by another – both flashing randomly into nooks and crannies. Jamie places planks of wood across the joists and climbs in.

"This is ridiculous," I hear Emma grumble, her head and shoulders over the rim of the hatch.

"You could well be right, Emma, but this is something I have to do. Something is up here – the recurring dreams I have of climbing up here and waking with a chill down my spine must mean something."

"But they're just dreams, Jamie. The more you think that the house is haunted the more you will dream about it. You just have to get it out of your mind!"

"No. It's more than that. Today I could *feel* a presence. And it stank, boy it stank so bad. A presence was definitely there – localised – right at my side. If I moved away into fresh air it followed me. I'm *amazed* you can't smell anything."

She rested her arms on the rim of the hatch and giggled. "Are you sure you hadn't just farted?"

"Ha-ha, very funny."

I emerge from behind the tank and wait as the dust rises from the insulation crammed in between the joists as he places the planks randomly to serve as stepping points. I will him not to fall though the ceiling – he is so close now.

He reaches the tank and shines the beam into the dry and rusty interior. I move toward him. His head jerks upright.

"It's here now, Emma!"

"I'm sorry, I can't smell anything."

"You won't from there; you'll have to come here!"

I see her pained expression. "I can't, I'm scared of falling through the ceiling. And I've never smelt anything before so I'm not going to now. I've told you, it's all in your head."

Her words enter my consciousness like a virus, only serving to weaken my link to the other side. The side I would still be on if I hadn't been pushed through the open trap door. I have tried so many times to make contact with her but I always fail to break down the barrier. She just continues with what she is doing, oblivious to my plight.

I move closer to Jamie.

"*Please*, Emma. It's here now, stronger than ever!"

She sighed. "Oh, all right."

Now at his side she sniffs the air. "I can't smell anything but a rusty old tank. You're going nuts."

She moved out of my presence and stopped. "That's odd." She shone the beam of her torch against the chimney. "Look at this, the mortar is a different colour on this part. And it's harder too; the rest is all crumbly and white. And look at the bricks at the bottom; they don't continue down through the floor like the bits each side of it."

My vision blurs as they move through me. Time shifts once again.

Many people are in the house now. The trap door to my sanctuary is open and a festoon of electric light fills every nook and cranny. Stepping stone planks have been replaced with large boards and I remain well away in the lowest of spaces in fear of losing my hook on the real world to yet another disturbance of my being.

Every brick removed from the fake chimney by men in white overalls evokes more memories – dreadful images of my demise from the hollow depths of my mind.

I see myself falling – reaching for purchase. The memory plays back in slow motion. My limbs flaying. The ladder toppling. The trap door ripping from its hinges. The blood running down my face from the impact with the banister.

I see my wife tower above me. Something in her hand – something heavy. A lump hammer.

"Oh, my God – it's a wrapped up body!" I don't know who said it. My memory and consciousness shatter.

More people are in the house now. Their images are obscure, their clothes dark. I can just make out the shape of a hammer as it is placed into a bag and sealed up. Everyone is talking but I can't make out what is said; the words are as hollow as my mind.

The vision dissipates, and time takes me away once again. But this time my world turns white. Calmness overwhelms me and a vision of traumatised faces form within a milky haze – best man and wife silently implore for forgiveness. Then they are gone.

White fades to grey, and grey to black.

THE TIES THAT BIND
by
Gareth Shore

Early Sunday afternoon ticks across the room from the mantelpiece clock. The television is switched off and dust motes drift in late afternoon sunshine filtered through the net curtains. George rests his mug on the newspaper on one leg, distracted by the heat burning through to his trousers. Too hot again. Not enough milk. They've plenty in; Mabel went for some this morning, not quite slamming the door whilst he was cleaning his teeth after having a lie in.

Across the room Mabel taps her wedding ring against her mug and glances out of the window, looking up through the net curtain. She notices the hedge between them and next door is poking out past the frame.

"That hedge of yours is getting untidy."

"Hmmm?" answers George, putting his mug down and staring at his paper.

"Untidy." Mabel is still looking out of the window. "You've nothing on tomorrow." And lets the statement hang there, each word underlined by the tick-tick-tick of the carriage clock on the mantelpiece.

Mabel leans forward slightly. "Sandra will be here soon." A quick look at the clock, then back to the window. "I'm ready." She waits.

"I was going to clip it back tomorrow," George says suddenly. "In the morning. Shed needs tidying as well so I'll do it then."

"Better get ready. Sandra won't be long now." She nods down at her bracelet watch, frowning briefly at blue veins showing through her skin. Thin skin. Suddenly wishing she had put her long sleeved blouse on, she rubs her arms and decides to get her cardigan when they set off.

George stretches, winces as a joint pops somewhere. "Better get ready," he announces and gets up, having to rock forward over the edge of his chair and push up with his hands on his knees.

"Your suit's hanging up on the back of the door with your tie. That nice silk one I got you. The red one."

George stuffs his bulky paper into the rack by his chair. "Think I'll wear the blue one this time. Not had it on for a bit."

Tick-tick-tick. "I hope that stain came out properly."

"It's fine. Dark blue. You can't tell, even if it is there."

Tick-tick-tick. "Well, Sandra won't be long now."

George steps on the rug as he crosses the room, his slipper squashing down the fur at one corner. He closes the door behind him.

Her eyes drift to the black and white photograph next to the television, the one where they pose, young and awkward, on a cold windy beach somewhere (Southport? Blackpool?) with the sea grey and flat and endless behind them. She goes over, fluffs up the corner of the rug, unfolds George's newspaper and slots it neatly back into the rack. Two strangers in the photo grin at her. *Is that really us? George had such smooth skin. And such dark hair. He always combed it straight back. Made him look slightly Italian.* Call me Georgio, *he'd joke,* the Lancashire lothario.

"Makes sure that blue tie's not stained!" she shouts up at the ceiling.

"It's fine. I've already got it on!"

Upstairs, George holds it in his hand. It looks past its best. A bit worn, a bit faded, but he has to wear it now.

A car crunches onto the pavement outside and stops. "Sandra's here," Mabel shouts a second before George does.

Sandra bounces through the door breathlessly and hugs Mabel, her voice loud in the small hallway. "They're nearly all there, mum! Place looks full already. The kids have been blowing balloons up all morning. I've left them there with Danny. Hi dad! You up there?"

"Hi San!" George comes down the stairs and smiles as Sandra kisses him on the cheek.

"You smell nice, dad. Watch yourself, don't forget Roamin' Rita's going to be there!" She pokes him on the lapel and straightens the folded handkerchief in his pocket.

George chuckles, puts his hands into his jacket pockets and shrugs. "Thought I'd try that aftershave you got me. Smells like the one I used to wear when me and your mum were courting."

Mabel, who has been frowning at George's tie, glances up at him in surprise. He is looking back at her. She coughs and rummages in her big brown handbag, murmuring "Keys". She inhales the scent quietly. And suddenly she can feel sand gritting between her toes. The sea is huge and flat all the way to the horizon, it seems. And dark blue shot through with green. A breeze rolls cooling over her hair and she realises that her hat has blown off, gone cartwheeling and bouncing along the beach. And there goes George, bounding after it, so light on his feet, his dark hair combed straight back, shouting. Her Lancashire Lothario. She bursts out laughing and runs after him, holding her skirt down.

"Mum? What have you lost?"

"Hmm?" Mabel looks up, frowning. George has gone to the door. Half hearing the sea, she says, "Thought I hadn't got my keys, but they're here." She glances at George, not quite silhouetted in the day glare, but just enough to hide the details and echo an outline she remembers well. She almost – *almost* - expects him to turn to her with a grin and slicked-back hair.

He does turn, but his face is wrinkled, his hair white and wispy as he pats his pockets, forehead creasing as he goes through his usual checklist: tablets; wallet; watch. Even a comb to tease the few strands left across his spotted scalp.

"Right you two, are you ready to meet your public?" Sandra jingles the car keys on the way out. "I'll steer you through the paparazzi. They've surrounded the club but we can get in the back way." She looks at the two of them standing together and smiles.

"Sandra, don't be silly. Go on, George, get in the front with Sandra."

George exchanges a brief look with Sandra, then walks out to the car and stiffly gets in the passenger seat. Mabel resists the urge to check the switches in the kitchen are off, takes the key out of the front door and locks it behind her. *That hedge really needs cutting back*, she thinks.

She jumps as Sandra toots the car horn. She smoothes down her skirt and unhurriedly closes the gate and gets in. "Right," Sandra announces as Mabel adjusts herself on the back seat, "let's go! Seatbelt on, mum."

"You've left something on the back seat, Sandra. An envelope."

"Yes! Good job you reminded me. I promised the kids you'd walk in holding their card!"

Mabel is quiet as she carefully peels the flap back and slides the card out. It is made of folded paper, but is stiff with big dollops and swirls of paint. It flakes onto her skirt but she doesn't notice. Two stick people (one has big curly hair) smile and hold hands on the front amid exclamations of primary colours. Underneath them is a big yellow circle (a wedding ring, she presumes) and a '50' in shaky orange. Wobbly red hearts form a border.

She holds it up to George in the front. He is also quiet as his eyes trace across the paper. Sandra is smiling in the rear view mirror. "It took them hours. They wanted it to be special." She turns the engine off. A silence fills the car.

Mabel opens the card. More wild colours and hearts. Another stick couple; this time the man is dressed in a grey suit and top hat and the woman is beaming in a long wedding dress painted bright white. Sandra's neat handwriting fills the rest of the space.

"They wanted me to tell you that they both worked on the card and did most of the colouring themselves. I had to do the writing, of course, but it's their words."

George clears his throat. Gives a little cough. "Read it out Mabel."

The silence is there again and George watches Mabel's eyes move from side to side, down, then side to side. Apart from the eyes, she is very still.

"Mabel?"

She doesn't look up but to George her eyes seem shiny in the gloom of the car.

"Here," she says. "You read it."

George takes the card and reads it.

"No," says Mabel quietly, "read it out loud."

Sandra reaches over and touches his forearm. "Go on dad. It's their words."

George takes in a long, deep breath. "Dear grandma and granddad, happy wedding anniversary. We hope you are married forever and ever from now on so we can have a million more parties. Lots and lots and LOTS of love, Declan and Ella."

George presumes the painted squiggles underneath are their names. There are lots of big black crosses.

Sandra breaks the silence. "They wanted to do fifty kisses, but ran out of room." She is still smiling.

George sits, head bowed over the card. He gently brushes a hair off it, very carefully closes it and hands it back to Mabel. She is staring at the envelope and George is still looking down, but their fingers still find each other, briefly touching. It is very quiet in the car as Mabel slides the card back into the envelope and carefully into her handbag.

George suddenly unclicks his seatbelt. "Don't start the car up yet, San. Forgotten my wallet."

"Oh dad! Everyone'll want to buy you a drink anyway, you know that."

George holds his grin, but his eyes flick to Mabel, who is holding onto her handbag in her lap with both hands. "Don't want the lovely Roamin' Rita to think I'm a cheapskate, do I?"

Sandra laughs. "Better empty your tin under the bed then. Remember, Rita only drinks doubles!"

George pushes himself out of the car and goes to slam the door. Mabel stops him with a "Keys" and gives them to Sandra to give to him. "Will you get my cardigan while you're there? The cream one with gold buttons. It's hanging up." Mabel sits back, lips pursed at the sky. "It said on the weather it's going to cloud over later."

Sandra gives George a toot when he gets outs and laughs when he jumps. He clutches his chest, mock-staggers, then waves, smiling, and goes into the house.

"I see you've got your good jewellery on, mum. Not seen that necklace for years. You'll blow Rita right out of the water!"

"All fur coat, no knickers, that one."

"Mum!" Sandra laughs out loud.

"Well."

"You know Rita used to fancy dad, back in his younger days. Said he looked a bit like that actor. You know, from those really old films they don't even put on telly anymore. Not even on Sundays."

"Rudolph Valentino."

"Yes, has she said before?" Sandra lets the silence return for a few moments. She looks out through the windscreen and says quietly, "You know that dad never gave her a second look."

"Like I say, all fur coat. George never went for that."

"He also says she never held a candle to you."

Mabel allows herself a brief smile and her look lingers for a second, maybe two, in the rearview mirror. "I know."

"Here's Rudolph now!" announces Sandra.

Mabel cranes her neck to see George struggling with the front door. He's forgotten you have to bang it or the lock sticks. He should have oiled it yesterday. She reminded him. His trousers are creased at the back of the knees. She can't see her cardigan in his hand, either. She sighs, taps her wedding ring against her handbag and frowns up at the sky.

Rudolph Valentino, she muses. *My Georgio.*

George turns and ambles down the path, definitely no cardigan in his hand. He stops to straighten his tie. It is that nice silk one she got him. The red one.

"Right!" he says as he gets in. "Andiamo!"

TRUTH

by

Esme Hewlett

I was a poor youth: with my wizened arm and the attacks of phlegm, I was of little use to my father. His Smithy needed all the help it could get, and while my brother had helped him from the beginning, I never could. Nothing was said but I could feel my father's shame and his sorrow. I tried to busy myself helping mother with the animals and the errands but I knew it wasn't enough. In these hard times after the poor harvests of the last few years everyone needed to work and I was more burden than help until my life changed forever that autumn day when the leaves were first starting to fall from the trees and the Priest came to the Smithy.

Often when he passed the Smithy the Priest stopped to sort the world out with my father. Father Swale had taken a liking to me in our occasional conversations just as I had taken a liking to him. He must have seen something in me; something past my wizened arm and my brother's cast off clothes. That day he offered me work helping him in St. Augustine's Monastery.

'We will feed and clothe you, pay you a modicum and if you take to the work we will teach you to read and write.'

'But I am happy here. I know nothing of Monastery life what if I cannot do the work?'

My father said 'You must go; Father Swale is a good man he will look after you. He would not have asked if he did not think you could do the work.' This is an opportunity of a better life. You must take it.'

My mother and father were overjoyed; both for themselves and for me. Not only would it mean they had one less mouth to feed but I could hold my head up and would no longer be the butt of the village jokes.. I knew it was a big change and I went with some apprehension but even then I did not know then what a giant step I was taking; I would see many things and move through a doorway into a very different world, a world not of poverty, hunger and hand me down clothes but of comfort, food and leisure.

Father Swale was a good teacher, I worked hard and I served my apprenticeship for some years before I became Chief Writer when Father Dominic's hand became too unsteady. I still kept my hobby tending the animals but now I had my own room, the scriptorium, in which I spent many happy hours copying manuscripts and writing letters for the Abbot. The Monastery and the nearby village lay astride the great north road from London to York and the wilder country beyond. Over the years many of the Lords and Ladies riding to and from London had been grateful to break their journey and stay with us overnight and sometimes even longer.

On these occasions, the Abbot would offer to show the most important visitors around the Monastery and its grounds. The scriptorium was often part of the tour and without exception the visitors were fulsome in their praise of our work. Richard, Duke of Gloucester, before he became King, stayed in the Abbots quarters several times, on his way to York. Though he never actually visited the scriptorium, and I only saw him from a distance, the Abbot said he praised my work highly.

When I first saw Richard close too he had been King for nearly two years and was on his way to Bosworth Field to fight the rebel, Henry Tudor. Richard was a big man and more impressive in the flesh than I had thought him at the Monastery those years ago. He toyed with his broad sword as if it were weightless. It was as though the strength from his weak arm had passed into his other arm, for that had the strength of both. He was standing on the steps of the Town House in Harborough Market Square, flanked by the banners of England and York. The front of the House, on the north side of the square, was warmed by the rays from the low morning sun and he looked very regal with the sun reflecting on his golden crown. It was only when I was closer that I saw that his armour was specially shaped for his crooked back and his wizened arm.

Even though it was early morning the square was crowded as locals gathered to watch his army march the six miles to Bosworth for the coming battle. I had never experienced the sights and sounds of such an enormous army before, the clattering of shoes on the cobbles and the smell of horses was overpowering. There was a festival atmosphere with jugglers, musicians and street sellers weaving through the crowd. The army was loudly cheered as they marched through the Square. Foot soldiers and cavalry were followed by teams of horses pulling the new heavy cannons. There were gasps of awe at these, I doubt if any had seen them before, and then there were ribald shouts as the baggage wagons and the camp followers strolled across the square.

I had to leave before they all passed. I must be at Bosworth when the King arrived. He had ordered me from the Monastery to be his new Court Scribe; I dare not be late on my first day. I made good time, which was just as well: he called for me not long after. I entered his tent of gold cloth with some trepidation; who would have thought that a poor cripple would one day be spoken to by a king? He was alone in the tent and he spoke to me gently and quickly put me at some ease.

'Scribe, you have a most important role this day. You are to record the true facts about my kingship. If by God's grace we win on the morrow then you will write the pamphlets praising God and our victory. If, though unlikely, we do not prevail then you will provide your records to my Lord Buckingham, who will see the truth is told and not the scurrilous lies that it may please Henry to spread'

I took out my paper and ink and standing prepared to write.

'Sit, buffoon, you cannot write standing; you are allowed to sit in the presence of the King if need be' he said

'You will write exactly what I say, exactly mind. Let us start'

He spoke in a deep, authoritive voice. ' I was at Middleham Castle carrying out my duties as Protector of the North that day in April in the year of Our Lord, 1483 when the messenger brought the terrible news that Edward, my brother, the King was dead.'

'I am not going too fast for you am I?'

My arm was aching but all I could mumble was

'No My Lord.'

'The news came in the black of early morning by letter from Lord Hastings. He had written - Edward is dead; Queen Elizabeth has called a meeting of the Council to agree the coronation of her son Prince John. If John, the ten year old Prince, became King then there is no doubt whatsoever that the Queen and her Woodville family would rule in his name. I would be a danger to them; even if they let me live, they would ruin me.'

'Let me see that last part 'He ordered

'Change that sentence to – The Woodvilles are not royal they are only Gentry, there was no way they could rule. It was my duty to take charge. There that will sound much better.'

'There was no time to be lost. We set off before daybreak. The Prince, his younger brother and their Woodville master, Lord Rivers, were already on the road from Ludlow. I had to reach London first or intercept them on the road.'

'Let me see what you have written so far.'

I showed him my penmanship; I was relieved when he seemed pleased with it. He carried on.

'We were going too slowly, the roads were full of holes and mud; at this pace we would never catch them. I had to send a rider to my trusted Hastings, to ask if he could slow them down. The return messenger met us at Nottingham. God and Hastings be praised, he had done well; Rivers had stopped for the night at Stoney Stratford. Now it was possible to reach them, but first we had to halt at Northampton, we could go no further that night, the horses were finished.'

He was speaking rapidly: I could not ask him to slow; you did not speak to a King unless he spoke to you so I lifted my hand as though with cramp. The King, a sensitive man slowed down to allow me to catch up; when I was ready he started again.

'I sent to Rivers suggesting he wait so we could join escorts in Stony Stratford and set off together the following morning. When we reached London I took the Princes through the cheering crowds to my own London house. I would move them to somewhere more secure later. We could now have a Council meeting but this one would be to agree my Protectorate of the underage Prince. As long as I held the Prince there would be no coronation, he would not be crowned and I would be Protector and ruler of England as my brother, King Edward had wished. '

'I particularly want to make sure that part is clear. I will read it later. Now I think we will rest your fingers there, I have work to do. Wait outside'

As I left the tent his commanders joined him; I could hear him through the canvas.

'I will be in the centre with the cavalry on the right, Buckingham's men on the left and the Stanleys in reserve. What news of Buckingham? When does he expect to be here?'

I heard the reply 'He has just set out Sire; he expects to be here later tomorrow.'

I could feel the fury through the tent wall

'WHAT?' Richard shouted 'Get messengers to him, NOW, it could all be over tomorrow.'

'What news of the Stanleys?'

'They have arrived Sire and are setting up the reserve lines'

'God be praised' Said Richard his voice filled with relief 'Send your fastest messengers to Buckingham, appraise him of the urgency, there is no time to lose. We need his men now.'

He stormed out of the tent; you could see in his eyes that he was furious with Buckingham.

'Get in here scribe?' He shouted.

Richard swore 'Damn I cannot concentrate. Where were we? 'Ah, yes change 'As long as I held him....to   He would be safe under my protection.' Then continue with - I transferred the Princes to the Tower for their safekeeping. Unfortunately the plague took them; it was particularly bad that year. We had to bury them in lime. With them out of the way   No change that to - After their sad loss I was the rightful hereditary King and later that year I was crowned in Westminster.

It was difficult not to let my feelings show for the news was abroad that Richard had had the Princes murdered.

Richard said.   'Now even after two years of stability and good rule we are here at Bosworth, about to fight off another challenger to my birthright. Henry, the bastard, comes to claim what he thinks is his inheritance. Well however many soldiers he brings here to Bosworth he will not take the Crown from me.

I will fight him to the end however bloody that may be.' ' Do not write that Scribe.' I nodded for, as I said, you do not speak to a King until spoken to.

'Before the battle tomorrow I want to see two perfect copies, with no crossing out, and I want you to guard it with your life.

That was the last time he spoke to me. Henry's attack started before Buckingham's troops had arrived and when the treacherous Stanleys refused to move from the reserve Richard was in a desperate situation being beaten back towards where I and his household stood. I saw his final charge, with his House Carls he drove through the lines directly at Henry himself. It was Richard's last act: he almost reached Henry but he was struck down by a mighty blow to the head rending his crown in two. Such a cry went up when he fell under the trampling hooves: it was as though the world had stopped at that very moment.

Both sides backed away from Richard's shattered body as a quiet descended over the whole of Bosworth Field, even the horses seemed to know it was the end. Dismounting, Henry was the first to move: he strode forward and with one blow severed Richard's head and lifted it into the air. The battle was over; Richard's troops turned and fled the field while Henry placed Richard's head on a pikestaff and held it aloft for all to see. Henry ordered the head and body to be buried in unconsecrated ground. Buried in secret, so that no one would ever find him: All that is left are the two perfect scrolls; but who now wants Richard's truth when they have Henry's?

JOURNEY TO THE WINDOW
by
Joanne Shaw

She needs to go. She has been lying in this darkness for long enough with the moon's steady light on the curtains calling her out. That first part, to the window, will take all her effort but she can do it; her willpower is strong though her body is not. She has made the journey to the window many times in her imagination, now it has to be done in reality.

She moves her quilt to one side and places her feet firmly onto the floor. There is no pain but there is weakness and a worry that her legs will not bear her body's weight – though, she thinks ruefully, there is not so much weight to bear. She moves slowly, holding onto the bed, then onto the leather chair (seen dimly outlined in white), then leaning her weight against the wardrobe doors and then onto the windowsill. The sill is broad so she half-sits on this a while, looking out. The grasses below must be waist-high – they are growing rampantly, healthily, and shine with the moon's reflected light. If she could reach them, their softness would support her while she rested, until she could go onwards, through the gate and out into the world. With a huge effort, she undoes the latch, pushes up the window and leans out, feeling below the ledge for the ladder she knows will be there.

As Tom opens the bedroom door, a cold draught hits him in the face. Through the chill and the blackness (there is no moon tonight) he notices Alice, quite still, over by the window, hanging half-in, half-out. He does not know what she is doing – he never has known what is in her mind but never more so than in the past few months – but he knows enough to be careful of her and so, putting down the cup of cocoa he has brought for her on the table by the bed, he moves as stealthily as a big man can towards her.

He reaches her, pulls her to him, away from the open window, and holds her in his arms. With one arm, he untangles the nightdress that has wound itself round her legs, then he carries her back to their bed. Putting her in gently, supporting her back and head with the plumped-up pillow and covering her with the quilt, he turns on the lamp.

'What was all that about, Alice?' he asks.

She feels too tired to answer, just looks at him with her dark eyes. She has beautiful eyes Tom has always thought, though he has never told her so. He waits. She speaks at last, though not expecting him to understand.

'I need to escape.'

'From what?'

She does not answer.

'Where did you want to go to?' he persists.

'Somewhere different from here, somewhere out of the ordinary, somewhere strange, somewhere – other.'

'Isn't our own place enough for you, then? We've worked together to make it nice – good furniture; wooden floors; a new kitchen – and what about the extension? You said that made it special.'

She puts her hand on his. 'It did ... it does,' but her eyes did not look into his – they were turned sideways towards the window. 'Our house is lovely – but I want something more.'

'You've got to be practical,' he tells her, 'particularly now. And anyway,' he continues, 'really, Alice, did you think you could climb out of the window and reach the ground?' He smiled at her ruefully. 'There's not even a tree for you to clamber down.'

'There's the ladder,' she says.

'What ladder? We don't have a ladder.'

He hands her the cup of cocoa. It is cold now but she sips it anyway.

Downstairs, he rinses her cup under the tap and places it upside down on the drainer. He worries that she will try something similar, something silly, tomorrow. She is too tired to do anything tonight. Perhaps he should have taken her on an exotic holiday while he could, to America – Florida, say, or New

York, even South America; she would have loved to trek to that place in the jungle, Machu Picchu. He had always been the one to hold back. He liked to be surrounded by the type of people he knew, places he knew how to behave in, places where he knew what was likely to come next.

At exactly half past ten, as usual, he makes his way upstairs. Alice is still awake and seemingly logical as she at least has her eyes on a book rather than on an escape route. He goes through his routine of getting ready for bed – wash, teeth brushed, pyjamas taken from underneath the pillow and put on – then slides carefully into bed beside her.

'Right. Talk to me,' he says.

'I'll try.' She puts down her book. 'I want to go where I've always wanted to go – somewhere glamorous, on a cruise perhaps, where you have to dress for dinner. I'd like to wear a special dress. I'd like to lie on a sun lounger while I watch the other passengers enjoying themselves, and then I'd look past them over the waves to see ships like dashes on the horizon.'

He doesn't state the obvious – that the best way to do that would be to book a place with a travel agent and go by car or train to the port – not drop through the window in your nightie without any luggage, passport or money. Neither does he state the other obvious – that she is not well enough to make that journey, or any journey.

Instead he says, 'All right. I'll see what we can do. I'll arrange something tomorrow. Go to sleep now.' She looks at him – is it in wonder or disbelief? He is not sure but then she turns onto her side. He turns off the light.

The next morning, Tom is already awake as the light seeps around the edges of the curtains. Alice is mumbling in her sleep but he cannot tell what she is saying. When he puts his hand on her forehead it is damp and, at eight when the alarm goes and she wakes up, her gaze is abstracted though she still smiles at him. However, Tom has had an idea and he is determined to realise it. He brings her some breakfast: fruit and yoghurt, toast and tea, and puts the radio on. She likes music; she says she cannot concentrate on the news.

'Back soon,' he promises.

Two hours later and he has brought back two black bin-liners. Out of one, he pulls, triumphantly, a long white linen dress; a shawl, soft and patterned with yellow flowers and with a green fringe, and a pair of green, strapped shoes.

'For your cruise, my lady,' he explains.

She pulls herself up and strokes the shawl's fringe.

'From the charity shop', he says. 'The woman there helped me to look for what I wanted. I couldn't find you a sun-lounger. Well, there was only a plastic one with wipe-clean covers and that didn't seem enough. But, and you'll never credit this, I've found a photograph of your ship, the *Clipper Adventurer*. And for the cocktail hour and the Captain's Dinner ...'

He upturns the second bin-liner. Alice leans over and takes the item that is uppermost. Shaking it out, she sees it is a red cocktail dress. Beneath that, there is a tiny hat with a net with dots on it.

'To cover your eyes so that you can watch the other passengers without them noticing you're looking!'

'You've thought of everything,' she says softly.

'Is that a sigh', he wonders aloud, 'of content or of sadness?'

'What's this?' She finds a kind of long furry animal.

'It's a stole, to put around your shoulders, to keep you from getting chilled in the evening. Look. You clip its tail into its mouth to fasten it. Don't worry, it's not real fur, it's nylon, the woman said.'

Alice leans back against the pillow. Tom can tell by her expression that she is pleased.

The next morning, Alice wants to be ready. Tom helps her into her white dress, uncovering her long, similarly white, feet to strap on her green shoes.

'They are beautiful but I don't think I can walk in them.' She considers the heels. 'They are very slender.'

156

'No matter,' he responds.

He wraps the shawl around her. It covers the fine bones of her shoulders. He puts Britten's *Sea Interludes* on the CD player and, as he goes downstairs, leaves her watching the sunlight as it glints against her glass and water jug. When he brings her lunch, she is asleep with the sun now shining full on her face. He opens the window slightly to let in a sea breeze.

By early evening, the light fading, it is the hour for cocktails. Alice manages to wriggle into the red dress; together they smooth it down till it falls loosely just below her knees. Tom fastens the fur stole across the top of her arms and a sequinned necklace across her throat. She reaches for her hat.

'First, can you put my hair up?' she asks him.

Having watched her do this many times, he gathers her hair into a band, twirls it and pins it with the long pins that always look so sharp and cruel. He brings her the mirror so that she can place the hat precisely on her head. It looks – right. She laughs. Together they have done well. He brings her a cocktail – pale green with a cherry.

'I didn't know you could do that,' she says admiringly.

'Only one of my hidden talents,' he replies, grinning.

She does not want the canapés he has made (another of his talents, unknown till now), as she is not hungry.

'But they look wonderful', she admits. 'Perhaps later.'

When night arrives and whilst she is resting, he brings in candles, lots of them, slender and cream, in tall bottles. He puts them all around the room. They illuminate his face, and hers, as he places each one. He thinks, just for a moment that, surrounded by candles, she is like Juliet lying on her bier. Then the flickering lights suggest movement and, indeed, she *is* moving and she appears, as she used to and as he hopes she will be soon, lively and sparkling.

She watches as the candlelight accentuates the lines on his forehead and the dark circles under his eyes and thinks, nevertheless, he has never looked so handsome and so dear.

'And now', he says, 'for some music.'

He puts on a slow waltz and, holding her firmly to him and supporting her almost fully, they dance around the room. The little flames catch on her sequins as they pass by.

The morning after, when he brings her tea and toast, she is unexpectedly already awake.

'Today,' he says, 'is the day we reach our destination. Prepare yourself.'

She laughs in anticipation. 'What on earth can be coming next?'

'I've just to pop out for an hour. I'm taking the van.'

He returns later than expected and somewhat out of breath. He jams open the bedroom door. She is asleep again but looks better, untroubled. He struggles in with the shrubs and flowering plants he has brought from the Garden Centre: a hairy tree-fern with massive fronds; a kiwi vine with its green leaves turning pink and white; a palm tree with outstretched fingers; Himalayan honeysuckle, white and red with reddish-purple flowers; trumpet vine, bromeliads, orchids and passion flower, a guava – more and more until he has made a tropical paradise in their room.

The first thing she notices before she even opens her eyes is the smell - sap and greenness, heavy and potent, just as in a jungle, and overcoming all, jasmine, drenched with the sweetness of pineapple. Peering through her lashes, she notes the plants are there – it is not a delusion or a fantasy, the growing things are real and as green, fruity and flowery as they smell. The bedroom walls are no longer visible. All is luxuriant growth – emerald and jade, lime and olive with flowers hidden amongst.

And there is Tom, having to push through leaves to reach her. He is grinning of course. He knows he has done well. He breaks off a flower with purple petals and dark pink stamens and threads it through her hair.

'Still want to go down the ladder?' he asks.

'What ladder?' she replies.

UNFINISHED HOUSE

by

Anne Walsh Donnelly

Peter sits on the only chair in his lounge and stares at the Ladbroke website. He scans through the list of horses scheduled to run in the Grand National. Pythagoras. A horse with a name like that was sure to win. He logs in to his account and enters his password.

The doorbell rings. He ignores it. He runs his hand through his oily hair and glances at the scrunched bank letter on the floor. Thoughts whizz through his head. They wouldn't come on a Saturday, would they? Surely those wankers would give him a bit longer before re-possessing.

His phone buzzes. He grabs it.

I'm outside, reads the text message.

He leans his thin frame across the desk, pulls the window blind and sees his mother standing outside. His chest tightens. He coughs to try and loosen it as he drops back into his chair. What's she doing here? He clicks to confirm his bet, closes the laptop then goes to open the front door.

"Mam?"

His mother hunches one of her shoulders to stop the strap of her handbag falling down her arm.

Peter scratches the reddening skin on his forearm as he studies her face.

"Are you going to invite me in?" she asks, as she straightens her pencil skirt.

"What are you doing here?"

She hates the city, almost as much as he loves it. She hates the traffic, the noise and the smoky air. He looks past her at the silver Yaris sitting in his driveway.

"You haven't been home in months and you hardly ever answer the phone when I ring."

"How did you find the house?"

"Sat Nav, a great invention. I'm giving a speech at a psychotherapist conference in the RDS tomorrow. I thought I'd come a day early and stay with you for the night."

Peter notices she's wearing her therapist face as she speaks. It doesn't stop his mind from liquidising as she steps into the hall, no hint of a wobble in the tower heels she's wearing.

"Oh, Peter, the cobwebs," she says, as he bangs the front door shut.

They drape over the unpainted cornice. A bluebottle has given up his fight to escape and his hunter advances towards him.

"I'm dying for a coffee," she says as she marches through the hall towards the kitchen.

"Why didn't you tell me you were coming?"

"I wanted to surprise you."

He follows her into the kitchen and watches her survey the sparse room. Her eyes flitter from the stainless steel sink to the small fridge beside it. Then her gaze settles on the blind-less window and the kettle perched precariously on the windowsill.

"Where's your kitchen?" she asks.

"You're in it."

She scrunches her face. It reminds Peter of a goat. Then she glances at the small table he'd salvaged from the skip at work. She sits on the only chair in the room and drops her handbag onto the dusty laminate floor.

"You can't live in a house without a proper kitchen," she says.

Why the hell not? He asks - in his head. He's been living here for the last year without one. When his fiancée called off the wedding, the house didn't matter anymore. Then he and some of his work colleagues had gone to a casino after the staff Christmas party. He'd got lucky on the roulette wheel and at the blackjack table. The skin on the tips of his fingers tingled as he placed his bet. He'd felt himself go hard with the anticipation of a possible win. But he didn't tell any of his colleagues that.

Sex is the farthest thing from Peter's mind now as he pulls the fridge door open to look for the Nescafe. Good a place as any to keep the jar, he thinks as he hears her sigh in the background.

"I'll sort out the kitchen when I get a chance," he says.

His mother gives him the look she wears when she's trying to decipher the food labels without her reading glasses.

"We could go to IKEA this afternoon and I could help you pick out some nice units."

Peter bangs the coffee jar on the sink's draining board to loosen the granules.

"I've exam scripts to correct today," he says as he takes two mugs from the unwashed pile in the sink, gives them a quick rinse and dries them with a paper towel.

"Do you not have a proper tea-towel?" she asks.

He throws the sodden paper into the sink and glares at her.

"Not that I'm judging," she says and crosses her legs.

Peter grimaces. She claims she never judges. Always spouting that Carl Rogers stuff about unconditional positive regard. Even as a boy Peter could see that the words coming out of her mouth didn't always match her face. Maybe in her office with her clients it did. He always thought they got the best of her. Sometimes when he was supposed to be doing his homework he'd sneak out to her office door and listen to the muffled voices.

His pocket starts to vibrate. He digs in, pulls out his phone and swipes his finger across the screen. Then he scans through the race updates. Pythagoras has fallen at the first fence. He shoves the phone back into his pocket and scratches the side of his neck. Just as the water in the kettle bubbles, his eyes start to sting. He turns his back on his mother, tips some coffee granules into a mug and fills it with boiling water.

"I've no milk," he says as he puts the mug on the table in front of her.

She takes a sip. He wonders if he could get some credit in the casino tomorrow night. He'll be sure to make back his losses at the blackjack table.

"Walnut or cherry?" she asks.

He stares at her.

"What?"

"Which type of wood would you like for the kitchen units?"

"I don't have any money for bloody units."

She sneezes and brown drops of coffee rain down on the top of the table.

"No need to swear, Peter. Surely with the big salary you're on, you can afford a decent kitchen."

He grabs a mug and makes a coffee for himself. Would she show him some unconditional positive regard if he told her where his money has gone, he asks himself. He remembers the time he stole an apple from the parish priest's orchard. When she'd caught him eating it, she'd marched him straight over to Father Murphy. The priest had given him three decades of the rosary to recite and his mother had banned him from watching television for a whole week. Peter had cried that night in bed and wished his father was still alive. He wouldn't have thought taking an apple was such a huge sin.

He gulps back his coffee; it sticks on the root of his tongue. His mother gets up and puts her mug on the draining board patterned with brown stains.

"What are you doing with your money that you can't put in a proper kitchen?" she asks as she stares out the window at the concrete block wall that separates his house from the next.

"My teaching hours have been cut. I've only been working half-time for the last few months."

"Why didn't you tell me? I could have helped you out."

"I didn't want your help."

She turns to face him. He notices that the lines at the side of her eyes have multiplied since he saw her last.

"Have we grown that far apart?" she asks.

He shrugs his shoulders and her tight face slackens as if there's something softening. But maybe he's imagining it. Still, the lines don't look as deep as they did moments ago and despite everything she is his mother. He remembers what she'd said after his father had died.

"I've taken out a life insurance policy," she'd told him. "I want to make sure you're looked after if anything happens to me."

He'd ran to his room, crying. At the time it wasn't money he wanted. But now?

"C'mon, I'll show you the rest of the house," he says.

When they reach the top of the stairs she squeezes her nose with her thumb and forefinger.

"What's that awful smell?"

He pulls the bathroom door shut.

"I don't smell anything."

She walks towards his bedroom, then stops. He watches her glance at the single unmade bed, sitting on the unvarnished pitch pine floor and the MDF locker he bought in Argos.

"You really do need some help," she says.

"Why bother with the house? It's not as if I'm going to get married anytime soon."

"Don't shut yourself off because of one failed relationship."

Peter glares at her as he stuffs his hands into the back pockets of his jeans.

"There's been more than one failed relationship."

"Some can be repaired. I had a client recently, he reminded me of you."

Peter grunts. The last thing he needs is to hear about one of her bloody clients.

"This particular client lost his mother, when he was twelve. It got me thinking of what it must have been like for you when your father died."

Peter takes his hands out of his pockets and clenches the top of the bannister as she moves closer to him.

"A bit late to be thinking of that now," he says.

"I know I wasn't there for you the way I should have been but I was so busy working trying to pay off the bills, your father left behind…"

"Don't blame Dad."

Peter lowers his head and looks down the stairs at the charcoal tiles below.

"I just want to say sorry for not being the mother you needed."

She reaches out to hug him. He steps back. Then words tumble out of his mouth before he has a chance to censure them.

"Sometimes I used to wish I was one of your clients, just to have one hour with you that you'd sit and listen to me."

"I'm here now," she says as she grasps his limp hand.

He shakes it loose and drags it through his hair.

"Please … I mightn't have always shown it but I do love you," she says.

He smirks.

"What if I told you I was in debt? Would you love me then?"

He raises his head and sees the expression she used to wear when his father came home from the greyhound track on Friday nights.

"You think I'm just like Dad, don't you?"

"You're not, I won't let you…"

"I'm not one of your clients, you can't fix me."

"There's nothing wrong with you. I just want to help you finish this house."

She puts her hand on his shoulder. He lets it rest there, feels the heat of it. Maybe they could finish the house together, he thinks.

"And I'm sure you'll get more teaching hours next term. I'll help you out with the bills till then."

Peter paints a smile across his face.

"Thanks, Mam."

Then he feels a dull thud on the floor of his heart and sweat trickles across his palms. The click-clack sound of a spinning roulette wheel is in his ears and the smell of shuffling poker cards is in his nose.

"I could go to IKEA tomorrow while you're at your conference," he says. "If you give me some cash,

I'll be able to put a deposit on some units if I see anything nice."

She gives him the hopeful look he'd often seen her give his father. But he's not like his father, he thinks. He'll win tomorrow when he goes to the casino. He's sure of it.

THE HONEY TRAP

by

Jacqui Cooper

I took a deep breath and rang the doorbell.

A man answered. Of course I'd known the client was a male when I took the job, but in truth, I much preferred to work with women. Still, a job was a job.

He was nervous; a newbie I guessed. At least he looked clean.

'Hi,' I said brightly. 'I'm Clare. From the agency?'

His Adam's apple bobbed as he swallowed. 'Yes. Of course. I'm Scott. Please, come in.'

I followed him down the hallway into the lounge.

'So how do we do this?' he asked.

'First of all, you relax.' I smiled. Putting clients at ease was part of the job. 'Then you tell me exactly what you want and I decide if it's acceptable. If it is, I lay down the ground rules. Then if we're both happy, we go ahead.'

He nodded. Licked his lips. 'How exactly do we...?'

'Let me worry about the details. So?' I prompted.

He took a deep breath. 'I think my wife is cheating on me.'

I'd figured it was something like that. It almost always is. 'And you want someone to catch her out? I hate to state the obvious, Scott, but surely a man would be better choice to entrap-'

He shook his head, more confident now. 'I'm not trying to trap her. I'm pretty sure I'm right and I'm pretty sure I know who with.'

Scott looked like a nice guy. A little overweight, maybe but not bad looking. Judging by the house and the car parked outside, he could easily afford my services and I really needed his money. But still... 'If all you need is proof, then a private investigator would be cheaper-'

He shook his head again. 'No. I need to see for myself...I have to be one hundred percent certain before I do anything.'

I could understand that. 'Who is it?' I sympathised. 'Best friend?'

'My brother.' Scott went on to tell me an all too familiar story. For years his wife had complained that he was always working and he never had any time for her. But now he had sold his business and had lots of time on his hands, she seemed to have very little for him. His brother too, was avoiding him on the flimsiest of excuses. There had been secret looks and too many coincidences. 'I don't have any other family,' he explained. 'If I accuse them and I'm wrong, I lose everything.'

I knew all about loss. Of course it wouldn't be professional to tell Scott that my fiancé had killed himself after he'd been swindled out of the business he'd poured his heart into. But I did know what it meant to be alone. 'We only have four hours,' I warned him. 'Is that enough time?'

He nodded. 'She's at a party tonight. A work thing at the Hotel Vincent in town. It would be easy enough to come home but she decided to stay over so she could have a drink. As if I wouldn't have picked her up or sent a taxi. I'd arranged for Dan – my brother – to come round for a few beers tonight. Unfortunately, something came up suddenly and he had to cancel. Again.'

Well, I suppose I'd be suspicious too. 'Okay, this is how it works, Scott. You wear my body for four hours. No touching anything you shouldn't. No looking at anything you shouldn't. No drugs. Clear?'

He nodded.

'I mean it,' I said sharply. 'If you do anything even slightly inappropriate, I dump you and you're card is still charged.'

'I wouldn't,' he said, sounding hurt. 'I'm not like that.'

Yeah right. They all said that. I'd had some doozies in the past. Men who didn't grasp how the Double Body process worked, and who thought they had my body free and clear for the whole four hours and that I'd have no memory of the fun they'd had with it. You don't even want to know.

Five minutes later it was done. I'm used to how the machine works now but of course, this was Scott's first time. I could feel him bouncing around inside my brain. 'Are you okay?' I asked. When I spoke, my voice echoed inside my head. When he answered, he spoke with my voice.

'W…what? How…?'

'You'll feel disorientated,' I said patiently. 'Move your...*my* arms and legs a bit, then try and stand up.'

He did and almost toppled over. Male clients often did that. I'm pretty well endowed and the boobs throw them off balance. He swayed, caught himself and we were off.

'Close your eyes,' I told him and he did. We bumped into the coffee table.

'His,' I sighed. 'Close *his* eyes.'

We looked at his body slumped in an armchair. It looked...empty.

'Your eyes will be gritty as hell if you leave them open,' I explained.

He leaned over and closed them.

'Take your phone,' I said and reminded him to lock the doors. His body was completely vulnerable in this state. If anything happened, he couldn't protect himself.

Stumbling, tripping and swearing, we made it to my car. It had to be mine; car insurance for body doubling was a very grey area.

Scott couldn't get the key in the door. And he could barely get himself into the car. There was plenty of room - the problem was his six foot two consciousness squeezed into my five foot two body.

'Shall I drive?' I offered. 'That way we might at least get there in one piece.'

At the hotel bar we engaged in a brief squabble over drinks.

Scott wanted beer. For his nerves, he said.

'Wine,' I insisted. I can't hold beer. 'No way are you taking my body to the loo.'

Glass in hand, we found a table where we could watch the goings on. Thankfully no one hit on me, which could have been awkward. I'm not bad looking but I suspected the combined Scott/Clare look and muttered one way conversation made us look slightly deranged.

His wife wasn't here. Nor was his brother and we settled down to wait.

'So how long have you been doing this?' Scott asked.

'Take your phone out,' I told him.

'What?'

'Take your phone out. Pretend you're talking to someone.'

'Oh, right. Good idea.'

He did and made a huge show of dialling a pretend number. 'So, how long?'

'We're not here for chit chat, Scott.'

'I know. But we could be here a while.'

He was right. Reluctantly I played along. 'A few months.'

'Do you like it?'

Actually, if he dug around in my brain he would know everything there was to know about me. It was a potential hazard of the job and I'd learned some strategies to protect myself. *Think about puppies and kittens. Don't let him in any deeper.*

'You're an animal lover,' he said. It was unsettling how quickly he had tuned into my thoughts.

Some clients never did. 'I always planned to get a dog once I had more free time.'

A wave of sadness washed over him and into me.

'You don't know she's cheating,' I said gently. 'And you can still get a dog.' A picture of a Labrador we'd had when I was growing up sprang into my mind.

'A black lab,' said Scott. 'Good call.'

He could read my thoughts almost before I thought them. Damn. I cast around for something to distract him. 'Tell me about your business.'

He shrugged my shoulder. 'Not a lot to tell. Buying and selling. Not very interesting, but very profitable.'

So I was right: Scott had money. And his wife would probably walk away with half in a divorce.

'Probably,' Scott agreed.

He was just too quick. 'Can you see her?' I asked briskly.

He looked around. 'No.'

'You sure this is the hotel?'

'I'm sure.'

On my suggestion Scott walked us to reception and asked them to call her room. No reply.

I knew I didn't have to point out that they could both be in the room and too busy to answer the phone.

'The clock's ticking,' I reminded him. 'Why don't you ring her?' Neither of us could think of anything else, so he did.

She was slow to answer. 'Who…who is this?'

It was Scott's phone. Why would she think anyone other than Scott would call her on it?

I told him what to say.

'I found this phone,' he said with my voice. 'I'm looking for the owner.'

'It's my husband's,' she said. 'W…where are you?'

'Where are *you*?' Scott countered, and I gave him a mental high five for his quick thinking. 'I could bring it to you.'

'I'm at the Hotel Vincent,' she said. 'In the bar.'

Oh no she wasn't. Alarm bells rang.

'Hang up!' I said urgently.

'What?'

'Just hang up!'

He did, looking round. 'So where is she?'

'Scott you have to listen to me. You could be in danger.'

'I don't see her-'

'Scott, she's not here. And neither is Dan. This place…booking the room…where do they think you are tonight?'

'At home watching TV. Getting drunk on my own.'

'They've set up an alibi, Scott.'

'For what?'

'I think they might be planning to kill you.'

I had no idea what would happen if he died inside me and I had no intention of finding out. 'Don't you get it? They're at your house. That's how she knew it couldn't be you on the phone. Because she's looking at you right now. And you're unconscious. There isn't time to drive-' Inspiration struck. 'Grab my boobs.'

'What?'

'Just do it, Scott.'

We were in a public bar but my urgency must have reached him. He did as he was told and just like that, my body was mine again.

Ignoring the stares I ran outside and jumped in the car, driving like a maniac.

Outside his door I took a deep breath and knocked. Mercifully, Scott answered. He had blood on his forehead.

'Are you alright?' I demanded.

He nodded.

'Where are they?'

'Gone. They ran off when I woke up yelling and swinging.' He touched his forehead. 'I fell over.'

In the lounge I saw a rope. Whisky. Pills.

'I think they planned to make it look like suicide,' said Scott.

Anger flooded my veins. Presumably Scott's wife didn't want to settle for half his money. 'Pity you can't prove anything.'

He smiled for the first time since I'd knocked. 'But I can. Nanny cam. It recorded everything, including their conversation as they argued how to do it. They're going to prison.'

'Nanny cam?' I was affronted. 'You didn't trust me?'

'I'm a suspicious guy.'

Not suspicious enough.

At home I wrote down the offshore bank account details I had located in his memory as we sat at the bar. It would probably take me a day or two to strip them all.

I would never get my fiancée back but the man who had defrauded him would never enjoy his money.

I'm not a killer. I'm glad I saved him. I wished Scott a long, long life.

Alone.

CUTTING THROUGH
by
Rachel Sargeant

Like homemade soup, the pool steams on a September morning. Michael could do with the water being cooler for training, but he never tires of the honey warmth growing up his thighs and on to his hips and chest as he lowers himself through the mist.

Out of the corner of his eye, he senses someone in the next lane looking at him. Although he's used to it, it rattles him. The other swimmer must be new. How many sessions will it be before he stops gawping. He dips under the water and swims away, hoping the guy will go back to his own training.

He completes a warm-up and is soon in his stride. He's home. Gone are all the knots that bug him: the nosey bloke in the next lane, the imminent pool closure, the stupid Sharks Squad idea. All gone, ebbed away. He presses on faster and becomes a human piston, tilting his elbows higher and piercing the water in front of him with the side of his hand. People talk about swimmers ploughing up the lane. He tills it, creating furrows of bow waves with his front crawl. As his arms sweep below his body in a lazy "s", he can feel the lift of the water against his hands like air against wings. It isn't just his own strength pushing him through; the water is working with him, carrying him forwards. Water is simple. If you slice it right, spear it like a javelin, it buoys you onwards. But if you slap it, it slaps you. Water doesn't discriminate in any other way.

He lunges at the wall and pulls himself up to check the clock. He's inside his personal best for 500 metres, but its half his usual distance so no big deal. His shoulders and chest, warm from the exertion, prickle; the guy in the next lane has stopped swimming too.

Michael drops under the water and holds his breath. When he surfaces, the man - a boy really - is swimming up the lane. He's lifting his head too high when he breathes but otherwise he's doing a decent stroke. He's a cut above the weekend wasters who usually bother Michael. If it hadn't been for Sarah, he would have long since binned the Sunday sessions. Too many louts in cut off denim, wanting to act the idiot with him. But Sarah made him face them, take them on. They're all the same. Water slappers, the lot of them. Heads out of the water, tossing from side to side. They never stand a chance against Michael's sleek lines. The same yob never tries it twice.

He used to say competitive swimming wasn't for him. And yet those petty victories gave him a taste for it. The elation of hitting that end wall and then, eyes still thundering with blood and adrenaline, managing to make out that no other swimmer has hit it ahead of him.

A thought squirms through his body and his stroke loses its rhythm. Why did they have to ask him to coach the Sharks Squad? Haven't there been enough breakthroughs in his life? Coaching would mean being on poolside. He told them straight he doesn't coach. How can he?

He tips back his goggles and looks at the sky. The sun is stirring behind the clouds. Autumn won't last beyond the morning; summer still owns the rest of the day. Why is the council closing this outdoor pool at the end of the week? He'll have to go back to swimming in the indoor "drain". The access is diabolical; the letter of the law not the spirit, and it's only a twenty-five metre pool.

That first winter he started swimming, he told Dad he wanted to give up until spring. He'd never master all the turns in such a short pool. Whenever he banged into the wall, the pain jabbed through his thighs and lasted for days. And the car park was too far away. The jagged air froze his hair before he got back to it. His dad's response was simple: he gave him a woollen hat, and as for the turns, well…

He takes the length on his back, the continuous motion of his arms folding the water under him and propelling him onwards. At the end he twists to his front without slowing down, dips at the hip and emerges on his back to start the next length: the perfect tumble turn.

Sarah and the kids will miss the outdoor pool, too. They've had a great summer. The twins can manage a width now and Danny is out of arm-floats.

Michael was seventeen before he started swimming. One of Dad's ideas, thrown up in desperation like all the other suggestions at that time.

"It's time you got off your backside."

He hated his dad then. How could someone who claimed to love him be so cruel? The first time, when he hit the water, his trunk sank to the bottom, dragging his head under. He came up coughing and retching. He wanted to make Dad sorry. He'd expected too much. But Dad stood there - watching him flail and claw - with his arms folded and face like glass, making no attempt to get him out.

Lads weren't supposed to cry, not even lads like him. He'd lived, hadn't he? What about the other two? So much for the "joy" of joy riding.

So he started swimming three times a week, not just the special session but public lane time too. Length after length he swam and length after length he balled his eyes out. Everyone thought he'd found himself with his new hobby, but he just came to blub into chlorine.

He flips on to his front and throws his arms over his head. His hands push hard through the water, forming a keyhole shape below him. With a monumental effort, he throws his arms over the water again. Despite his upper body strength, butterfly always hammers him; no leg power for the shoulder lift. He said once he'd never manage it but he's up to eight lengths now.

It was the same when he met Sarah. She asked him to be her training partner but he told her no. He didn't train. How could he? But she kept on asking. And so lap on lap, her breaststroke paced by his crawl. She suggested coffee in the pool canteen, later the ground floor wine bar in town. And he mentioned dinner.

He tucks in his chin and hefts his arms clear of the water for the last thrust to the end. Years of practice have perfected his timing and his hands land lightly on the wall. He pushes his arms away in an arc through the air, forcing his body on to his back. He sets off slowly down the lane, moving both arms together over his head.

He's relaxing into the cool-down when the lad in the next lane bobs up. Here we go. His shoulders stiffen, causing his arms to flatten. Even after all these years, whenever someone starts, he finds his skin tightening until it feels too small for him.

"I was wondering…" says the boy.

Michael takes a deep breath. That old chestnut. *I was wondering…* How many times has it kicked off with that?

"I was wondering if you'd look at my crawl. Tell me what I need to do."

The boy hasn't realised. He's just seen him speeding through the water like any other swimmer. Michael tells him about not lifting his chin to breathe.

The boy sets off and, following Michael's instructions, keeps his head down on the water. His stroke improves and he completes the length at speed. Michael suggests some front crawl drills.

"Cheers," the boy pants afterwards. "You're a great coach."

Coach? For a moment Michael feels like keeping up the pretence that the boy has assumed, but he waves to the lifeguard, pushes himself up and twists round to sit on the poolside. He stares down at the other swimmer, waiting for the look of revulsion to cross his face.

"I'll get it for you," the boy says, hauling himself out of the water.

He pushes his good foot to the ground and stands up, his arms outstretched to keep his balance. He limps to the lifeguard, dragging his withered leg, and returns, pushing Michael's wheelchair, letting it support his weight.

"I'm in Sharks by the way. We're looking for someone. So what do you reckon?"

SITUATION VACANT

by

Deborah Came

The Four Horsemen of the Apocalypse are looking for a fifth...

Pestilence scratched behind his ear, leaned back in his chair, casually glanced down at his broken, blackened fingernail to see what he had managed to scrape up. Something small wriggled over his hand, past his wrist and up into the sleeve of his dirty robe. Mid-afternoon and the interviews had been going on all day. If he heard one more person talking about how their team-working skills married well with their ability to work independently, the need to foster self-esteem, to give anything more than 100%, how their main fault was that they worked too hard... He knew he was old-fashioned but he still could not see the problem with just choosing someone at random and training them up. *Tabula rasa* approach. It had worked when they'd taken on Famine. He hadn't looked promising to start with but a bit of mentoring, and patience, he'd got the hang of it. Gut instinct, that was the key, thought Pestilence. Courage of your convictions.

"Sorry, did you say something?" The woman from Human Resources was looking at him with something approaching annoyance. Had he said anything out loud? He sighed.

186

"No, sorry, please carry on," he said, turning towards the young woman sitting on the hard-backed upright chair placed in the middle of the room. She was dressed smartly: mid-length skirt, matching jacket, although that had been hung over the back of her chair on this warm summer's day, crisp white blouse, only slightly marred where a pen had leaked down its front. Immediately opposite her, the Four Horsemen and the woman from Human Resources were ranged behind a polished ebony table, each with a pile of papers and a notepad in front of them.

The young lady cleared her throat and began to talk. Clearly she was very nervous: her voice was trembling, and he had the distinct impression that she was trying very hard to use her handkerchief to keep her nose covered while she was talking. It was true, there was a certain *fragrance* in the room. A full day of interviews, inefficient ventilation in an already warm space, and Death could be a bit whiffy. The rest of them had got used to it, but no good applying for this particular job if you were going to get queasy every time one of your colleagues was close by.

"I ... erm ... the thing is, I think what you should be looking for is, that is, it seems to me that you're missing a particular skillset ... Um, could you repeat the question please?"

War was sitting in the middle of the interview panel, immediately opposite the unfortunate candidate. He looked cross. Not a good strategy, to wind him up at this point in the proceedings. "For the last time," he said, "Please can you explain what your particular strength is and how your skills will complement those of the existing Four Horsemen".

"People!" The woman from HR sounded exasperated as she said this.

"Oh bloody hell!" muttered Death. "It's political correctness gone…" He trailed off. They all knew what he meant. They all agreed with him. But times had changed. They were now the Four Horsepeople of the Apocalypse, or alternatively the Four Riders, but definitely no longer the Four Horsemen.

"… those of the existing Four Horse*people*", War continued, glaring in turn at the two female occupants of the room, as if it were their fault that the world had moved on in the way it had.

"I think that my particular skill…" the young woman began, fidgeting slightly with the folio that she held on her lap, with all her certificates and statements of learning and competence. Her fidgeting was clearly too much for the flimsy folder: as if compelled by its own energy source it slipped from her lap, fell onto the floor, and the papers within scattered over the floor, some in plastic sheaths appearing to skitter all the way to the corners of the room. The hapless candidate began to get up from her chair to gather up the papers closest to her feet, then slipped on one of her certificates, almost fell, righted herself, then half crouched, half walked around the floor picking up her hard-won papers as she went.

"Carry on," said War. "I'm sure you can pick those up and talk at the same time. *Multi-tasking*," he said, with a sarcastic leer at the woman from HR. She appeared not to have heard him.

"It's just that..." said the candidate, "it seems to me that at the moment your team is very, well, unsubtle..."

Death groaned, although it sounded more like a rattling, wheezing sound. "Un*subtle*! Nothing un*subtle* when we move in, I'll tell you..."

"Yes, alright, thank you Death," said War, frowning at his colleague. He had to admit, he had had similar thoughts about Death over the years, so he wasn't going to prevent the candidate from expressing her thoughts. "Can you explain what you mean?"

"Ok, well what I'm thinking is that each of your *skills*..." She smiled as she used the word, trying very hard to make eye-contact with each of her interviewers, although it was difficult when they all wore capes with such big hoods that their eyes were more or less hidden, merely faint red glows that burned with varying degrees of energy and malice. "Each of your *unique skillsets* is based on maximum impact on the greatest possible number of people at the same time."

"That's the bloody point," muttered Death. War ignored him.

"And I think that's *fantastic!*" the candidate continued, warming to her theme. She was still picking up papers, now towards the far corner of the room, where the slightly opened window gave her an opportunity for some deep breaths of fresh air. She picked up the last of her documents and stood up straight, facing the panel again. A button pinged off from her blouse; thankfully she had reinforced its opening with safety pins that morning, "But I think I can bring something that is less, shall we say, in your face, which can in itself cause a certain amount of misery and mayhem but when mixed with any of your skills – individually or collectively – can have a pleasing amplificatory effect." She hesitated. Was amplificatory a word? She wasn't sure, but none of them had reacted so she thought it best to carry on with the appearance of confidence. She tried again for eye-contact; she failed again. She walked back towards the chair, went to sit down on it, lost her footing and ended up on the floor, grasping her folio in one hand while she used the other to lever herself into a position from which she could stand up again. Once on her feet she rested one hand on the back of the chair, which immediately tipped over, falling onto its side with a loud, echoing clatter. "I think," she continued, "that I can genuinely claim that I can give 110%, because through 100% of my skills I can add at least 10% to yours." She smiled at them all, revealing teeth that had clearly had spinach or lettuce pass by them earlier in the day. She sat down – successfully this time – and reached for the glass of water on the table in front of her. It fell over, as if by its own volition, and sent its contents running towards her documents and those in front of each of the interview panel.

War gazed into the middle-distance. None of today's candidates had struck him as overwhelmingly good for the role, but each had their strengths and areas that could be worked on. This one, however, had a different way of thinking about things, and perhaps that's what they needed. Perhaps the time had come to change the way they did business. Millennia of success was one thing, but they'd all begun to get a bit *stale*, and he was getting bored, if he was honest. Glancing at his colleagues he could tell that they were thinking along the same lines. Pestilence had stopped scratching and was sitting in a position he could only describe as alert. Death was very, very still. Famine was tapping his bony finger on the table in a way that War knew meant that he was excited by something.

"That's interesting," said War. "Thank you. That is the end of our formal questions, so unless there's anything you want to ask us…?"

"Well, the holiday entitlement wasn't quite clear on the advert," the candidate began.

"I can fill you in on all that," said the woman from HR. "It's in the application pack…" She glanced down at the sodden papers lying on the desk, ink running into illegibility. "I'll send you a new one," she said.

"One more thing," said Death, leaning forward. "You may be surprised by this question but it's amazing how many people say no. If we were to offer you this job, would you take it?"

"Yes!" said the candidate and it was the first time that she had said anything without appearing to either hesitate or equivocate. "Yes I would!"

"Right, then, thank you for coming in, we'll be in touch very soon," said War, standing up to shake the candidate's hand. "It was very nice meeting you, Ms Chaos."

HELATIDE
by
Finn Arlett

There are many things I'm uncertain of, sitting here on this platform, but of one thing I'm sure: somebody doesn't belong here.

I steal another glance at the blonde-haired teen sat on the floor in front of me as he strums a tune on his guitar. His head is down as he watches his own fingers produce a melody that none of the rest of us enjoy. And yet, for his sake, we say nothing. He's not playing to pass the time; he's not even playing to impress us. I suspect he plays because the silence of this unearthly platform makes him uncomfortable, and he knows why he's here.

Beside me, curled up with her legs drawn into her chest, is a young woman. She rests her chin on her knees, keeping herself closed from everybody else. Her hijab is untidy. Strands of hair fall in front of her eyes as though she'd fixed her appearance in a hurry. Her expression is blank and I want to ask her how long she'll stare at that crack in the floor tiles for. She knows why she's here, but not the *reason*.

Alone, at the far end of the platform, sits a hunched figure in a black coat, turned away from the rest of us. He perches on a concrete block with his knees spread apart and his elbows rested upon them. I've been staring at him for a while now and he hasn't moved. I'm not even sure he's breathing. He's been here the longest and now he grows exhausted. This man knows why he's here, and he's waiting for the train like an old dog awaits its master's return.

The remaining two are a couple covered in blood. The man – in his early thirties and dressed in what was once a perfectly ironed suit – cradles his girlfriend. His fingers dig into the bruised skin on her arms, leaving pale circles whenever he readjusts his grip. The woman sobs under her breath; her grief is evident in the pink flush of her eyes and the way her hands fidget with the hem of her dress. She doesn't want to cry in front of her partner, but she knows why she's here and it's consumed her. I sense her boyfriend also knows why he's locked down here on this platform, but he's only fooling himself if he thinks he can undo his fate before the train arrives.

Lastly, I gaze at the announcement board for the Helatide and heave a sigh. What did I expect would change? There are no departure times, no stops, no destinations written in those LED letters. The announcement board has been broken since I got here. Behind me is the track that the train runs on: a single blue beam of light pulsating like the screen on a heart-rate monitor. I've never seen a train run on a track like that before and I have to wonder how it works. And where does it *go*?

Over to my left, the boy begins to hum to his tune. He's probably never heard himself sing before, or none of his friends and family ever had the kindness to tell him he's tone deaf. But the silence is worse. Still, none of us chide him. The bedraggled soul beside me bores her gaze further into the cracked floor tile, the couple a little farther away turn a deaf ear to the world, and the mysterious man at the far end of the platform hunches still as a gargoyle.

How much longer will this wait continue? I shouldn't complain; I only have myself to blame for being here. The whole adventure had been *my* stupid idea. I, too, know the reason I've wound up on this platform. I sense every one of us knows our situation even if we don't understand it, and yet something isn't right. One of us doesn't *belong* here. Why can't I get it out of my mind?

The man in the black coat gets to his feet and all heads in the room turn in his direction except for the teenager's. The man stands for a moment, listens, and his fists curl.

"Cut it out," he growls. I note his American accent.

The boy stops mid-strum and lifts his gaze. I make eye-contact with him and nod towards his guitar.

"About time," the man says.

"Who, me?" asks the boy. He sounds too cheerful. Too annoying. "Something up with my playing?"

"If you knew what kind of place this is, you wouldn't be doing anything at all. Just sit still, shut up, and wait for the train like the rest of us."

The boy puts his guitar down on the tiles with deliberation. "I *know* what kind of place this is," he replies. I have to commend his boldness. "I've known for two years I'd wind up here."

I lift my chin. "Two *years*?"

He shrugs. "Cancer," he says, and his gaze falls on the track behind me. His deep brown eyes flash with each pulse of blue light. Finally the man sits again, resuming his brooding.

"You?" the teen says to me.

"I guess I drowned," I answer. "I totally thought I could make it ..."

"What happened?"

The memory still brings me shame. I hope my friends don't blame themselves for leaving me behind. I hope my parents still find some pride in me even though I'd always been a reckless idiot. "I was ... exploring. You know, some caves off the coasts of Sri Lanka. Thought it would be fun to get high there; make a cool story of it when I returned home. The tide came in and my friends and I got trapped, and I ... guess I didn't get out in time."

"I'm sorry," he says.

I sigh again. "Shit happens."

"Careful what you say." The young woman beside me wraps her arms around her legs.

"What happened to you?" the teen asks.

"I don't want to talk about it."

"And where else can you talk about it?" grunts the man in the black coat. "We're all here for the same thing."

I touch the girl's arm. "You don't have to tell anybody, if you'd rather not."

"I never want to relive that moment," she whimpers. "Never. There was nothing I could do ... I couldn't save myself from them."

"Shh. It's okay."

"Hey," the teen says, turning to the distressed couple at the back. I cringe inside. How can he be so cheerful? "What happened to you two?"

The blood-covered man catches his girlfriend's eye before answering. "RTA," he mumbles in response, and hangs his head again.

"RTA?"

"Road traffic accident," the man in black interjects.

"I'm sorry," he says to them with a sad smile. "I'm sorry for you all, actually. You've all had a pretty rough time. As for me I knew I'd end up here and, sure, it was scary from the word go, but I've made the last two years count. I've said my goodbyes, done everything I wanted to achieve, seen all the places I wanted to see. No regrets. I'm sorry you all couldn't do the same."

I speak up. "Is that why you're so happy about being here?"

"I wouldn't say I'm *happy*, but I've accepted boarding the Helatide."

"So have I," says the black-clad man. "Don't mean I'm happy to be here."

"What happened to you?"

The man finally turns towards us. His face is hard and harsh, his small brown eyes piercing in the gloom. He's bald on top, though sports a grey beard and sideburns, and I spy the glint of a gold ring through his septum. "You wanna know what happened to me?" he half-chuckles. "Some guts you got, kid. Don't you know who I am?"

"Nope," the teen says. "You're American. I'm Austrian. *Should* I know?"

The man snorts. "Mauricio Talamantes. Name ring any bells with ya, kid?"

I take a sharp breath. "The Rosemont shootings ..."

The corner of his mouth lifts. "Damn right. Kid asks me why I'm here. You gonna tell him, or do I gotta spell it out?"

"You were on death row," I whisper.

"Yeah. Been on death row almost a decade. Still feel sorry for me, kid?" The boy shakes his head. "And so you shouldn't. Last thing I saw's that machine pump me with some lethal injection. Sure, I got some regrets outta it, too: regrets I got in too deep, regrets I've gotten myself caught. Regrets my little boy ain't gonna know his papa and end up just as bad as I am. But" – he leans in and rests his elbows on his knees again – "what can I do about it now? Time slows down in here, kid, an' when you're waitin' for that goddamn drug to kill you, days turn into weeks down here. You, Indiana Jones." He thrusts his chin at me. "You got regrets?"

I have to think about it. Nothing immediately comes to me. I was a privileged only child, did well in school, lived the party-life at university, failed, and travelled the world ever since. What was I missing? "I disappointed my parents, I guess," I tell him. "Drank too much, slept around, smoked stuff. Never made them proud; never got a chance to say I'm sorry for being an idiot."

He addresses the woman in the hijab. "What about you? You got a name?"

199

"Sisi," she mutters to the floor. "I just ... I wish I'd been able to see. I mean ... see the monster he was."

"What about you two lovebirds?" Mauricio asks the couple. I sense his question is not welcome, as the pair let it hang in the air. "C'mon. Ain't none of us gonna see each other again, and ain't none of us gonna get a chance to confess like this. Any regrets? I sure as hell ain't askin' again."

"I ..." the bloodied man begins, "I was driving too fast. We were having an argument. I wasn't looking where I was going and ..."

The woman in his arms speaks for the first time. "I don't hate you, sweetie. I didn't mean what I said."

"Well," says Mauricio, "ain't that cute."

"There's still something on my mind," I say.

"More regrets?" asks the teen.

"No." I run my fingers through my hair. How do I put this without sounding nuts? "We all know why we're boarding the Helatide: illness, murder, lethal injection, three accidental deaths. But one of us doesn't belong here and I don't know why I know it."

"I feel it too," says the boy, "as though something's wrong. Anybody else feel it?"

The woman beside me nods and Mauricio sighs with a heavy heart. The man in the bloodied shirt gives me a sad smile and nods, too. The only one on the platform who doesn't respond is his girlfriend.

"Is it you?" Mauricio asks her. His voice is not tender, though I can tell he tried. "You don't belong here do you?"

She sniffs and her eyes brim with tears again. "No," she says. "I shouldn't be here. I need to be at home –"

"I'm so sorry," her boyfriend whispers, burying his face in her hair. "I'm so, so sorry."

"You think *you* should be the one who escapes the one-way train?" Mauricio spits. "Like hell. You might be here by accident, but as Indiana Jones over there says: shit happens. Accept it. You're stuck down here until the train rolls in. Might as well make the most of what time we've got left in limbo."

"Not me," the woman sobs. Finally, after all this time, her partner lets loose his feelings and sobs.

And then I understand.

"Not me," she repeats.

I watch in horror as she rests her hand on the bump in her abdomen.

BLACK CATS
by
Julie Hayman

'Death sometimes comes as a black cat in the dark, yes?' Layla Kovač's accent gives the words an unfamiliar slant. She offers a nicotine laugh. The last remaining light cuts through the Venetian blinds, striping her face tigrish and casting long bars over the floor and chairs. Evening is muscling in, stripping the room of colour, turning it as grainy and deceptive as a black-and-white film.

'What kind of accent is that?' asks Cain. 'Hungarian?'

'Not Hungarian, no.' Layla's obsidian eyes hold him steadily.

'Can we have a light on?'

She gestures a graceful hand towards the fringed lamp on the side table near Cain. He reaches over and switches it on: it gives out a sickly glow that flashes and ticks with the obduracy of a migraine, throwing the rest of the room into deeper gloom. It gives the place the atmosphere of a séance.

In the blinks of light, Cain sees that she was once beautiful: the shadow of it haunts her face like a scar. She sits with bare feet curled up in the armchair, wrapped neat as a puzzle. She might be forty-five or fifty-five: it's hard to tell. Her hair is black, not grey, but the years and her profession are scribbled in the lines on her face.

'Witnesses saw you and Davis at the bar together,' says Cain. 'You were the last person to see him alive.'

'I imagine his killer was the last person to see him alive,' says Layla evenly.

'You are the last person *known* to have seen Davis alive,' Cain corrects himself. The room is getting cold; the fuel in the paraffin heater has run out. The fumes stick in the back of his throat like an awful medicine. Somewhere in another room, an air-vent slaps.

Layla shrugs. 'Davis came back here that night. We drank. He fucked me, then paid and left.'

'And he was found dead in the alley beside this building at six the next morning.'

Again, Layla shrugs. 'A tragedy, no?'

Cain's mobile phone beeps. He takes it out of his pocket, glances at it, turns it to silent and puts it back. 'Did you know Davis well?'

'No.'

'Witnesses say you met him at the bar once or twice.'

'That doesn't mean I knew him well.'

A siren wails outside as a police car dashes past, flashing lights skittering, chopped into cine film across the ceiling.

'What time did Davis leave here?'

Layla lowers her gaze, rubs her finger over a stain on her skirt; raises her face to Cain's again. 'It was past midnight.'

Cain becomes aware of a clock ticking in the room. The spent paraffin singes his nostrils, the pulsing light from the lamp makes his eyeballs sore. From the corner of his eye he catches a shadow moving stealthily along the walls. A black cat leaps out of the darkness onto Layla's lap.

******

She had told Davud to be quick. There was a rumour of bread and dried beans in the market place in the north of the province fifteen miles away and all the boys had been sent there at once, on pedal bikes, on carts, on foot, to barter and beg and steal what food they could. Layla watched the dusty road anxiously, her hand a visor shading her from the sharp light that cut like a blade. The road shimmered in the heat, and dust whirled as the breeze caught and spun it.

The fighting was coming nearer to the town each day; little pockets of it breaking out here and there, skirmishes which grew into battles which became the advance of war.

Soon they might have to leave, her husband said. *'And go where?'* Layla asked, *'Where can we go?*

'We will load the family and belongings onto the cart and head west,' Tarik said,' *someone will help us'.*

So that was Tarik's plan: to load Davud and little Hana and his tree-bent mother and Layla's weather-worn father onto the donkey cart and for them, Tarik and Layla, to take them to safety, trusting to the goodness, the generosity, the assistance of strangers. And if Tarik had doubts about this plan, he would not reveal them to Layla. He would not say that the bony donkey had an ulcer on her leg that would soon make her lame; he would not question the ability of his mother to endure the rattling ride on the hard bed of the cart; he would not glance daunted at the mountains that rose blue and vast as dreams to the west. Layla looked at his fine-cut profile and was glad he would not speak his fears. After all: what else could they do but flee?

Davud did not come home that night and nor did the other boys. The mothers gathered around the olive tree in the square and pretended to convince each other that the boys were safe, were on their way home, would arrive by first light or, at the least, soon after. When sunlight sat atop the tower, the boys would arrive. Or when the sun touched the top of the fence. Or certainly when the sun hit the well-hole, the boys would be home. The women no longer cared whether the boys brought food with them: they traded the thought of food for the boys' lives, and were glad of the bargain.

The sun split white as bone in the treetops the next day as a hurricane of dust appeared on the horizon. It was the boys coming home – no, it was too big a dust cloud to be the boys; the boys must have brought others, many others with them. Layla snatched up Hana, playing in the mud by the well, and hugged the baby close on her left hip. 'Tarik!' she called. 'Come see.'

Tarik came out of his workshop to the screech of jeeps and motorbikes and covered cattle lorries pulling into the square.

A big man in army gear got out of a jeep. He was tall, his hair a white mane, his nose a meat cleaver. 'Call out the men of the town,' he ordered. 'Line them up over there.'

The women flustered and fluttered, crying like night birds, weeping into the blanket folds of the babies they held, wailing over the heads of toddlers who clung to their skirts and themselves wailed. A handful of soldiers rounded them up and corralled them under the olive tree. Other soldiers, rifles in hands, tramped into the houses, prodding the men and old folk out into the scouring light, lining the men up along the road.

A sudden wind got up, flapping the canvas on one of the cattle trucks, lifting it, revealing boys, shoulders hunched, faces stiff with fright, their boys, bruised and bloodied, ten or twelve or thirteen years old. Davud, his eye swollen shut, cradled his arm as if it were broken.

Two soldiers gestured to the boys to jump down and join the line of men. They were marched off across scrubland to the northeast, the soldiers handing them picks and shovels, cracking with gun-barrels any skulls that dared glance back. The women howled.

'Quiet, you hags,' the cleaver-nosed man yelled. 'We'll be back to deal with you later.' He turned to the soldiers, laughing, saying: 'They don't look so good, but all cats are black in the dark, eh?'

Then the little ones were taken from the women, screaming, off away behind the civic building, the largest structure in town, where the cries could not be heard. Layla grasped Hana tight, doubling over her, but the soldier yanked Layla's hair back, elbowed her hard in the face, and wrenched the child away as if she were a sack of wheat.

One woman, Marit, broke free of the cordon and ran at the soldier who was carrying off her child. 'Josif, Josif!' The bullet spread her face so wide that, later, Layla found a tooth snagged in her hair.

******

Cain has no clues to Davis's killer. It seems to be the job of someone who knows about these kinds of things: how to kill, how to leave no traces. Davis had been split from groin to sternum with a butcher's knife, his entrails left messy as unravelled wool. The *why* was a mystery: Davis had been a quiet, unremarkable store manager who paid his bills and visited prostitutes only when he could afford to. He spoke nice; didn't rough them up; thanked them afterwards. There was nothing in his background to suggest he had enemies: a milder man would have been hard to find. Cain had interviewed all the pros Davis had been with, and was still no nearer to solving the crime, so here he is, back at the bar, going over the same ground again. He wants another word with the manager, just in case there's anything he's forgotten to mention, anything he's missed, and he's brought a head-and-shoulders snapshot of Davis with him, on the off-chance there's someone new to show it to who might recognise him and be able to cast light on the case.

'The manager will be with you soon,' the barman tells him, then goes off to serve other customers.

Cain sits at the bar, twirling a whisky in a tumbler, swigging its smokiness and brooding over the snapshot. Davis's *Mr Punchinello* nose dominates the photo. Davis – or at least that nose – reminds him of someone, but he can't think who. Hell of a hooter to have. Cain had a schoolmaster with a nose like that – though that's not who he's reminded of. Who is it? Someone on the news, from a while back?

That's when Cain sees her, the Hungarian hooker – *is* she Hungarian or some other nationality? – wearing a platinum blonde wig, propping up a pillar, waiting for a punter to come along and buy her a drink, buy her a bar meal, buy her. What's her name again? Layla. Layla Kovač. Light-haired now instead of dark, but it's her, all right. She sees him looking and sidles up.

'Hello, again.'

Close up, under the neon strip-lights of the bar, he sees that she's painted a Marilyn Monroe-type beauty spot above her lip. It looks like a small-gauge bullet hole in her face.

'I'm hungry,' she says. 'Buy me food.'

He leans across to attract the barman's attention, knocking over a salt cellar. Grains spill over the bar in incomprehensible constellations. 'Give her whatever she wants,' Cain says. 'I'll pay.'

Layla picks at the lasagne the barman brings, and pecks half-heartedly at the side order of garlic bread.

'Anything else you can tell me about Davis?' Cain asks.

'No, I don't think so.'

'Nothing at all?'

'No.'

Then Cain remembers the cat jumping from the darkness onto her lap in her dingy apartment, remembers her saying something about death coming like a black cat in the dark. There's no apparent motive and no sure evidence, but on a wild guess, he asks: 'Did *you* kill Davis?'

Layla's obsidian eyes glint. She puts down her fork and knife and leans towards him. 'Ok,' she says, 'For argument's sake, let's say that I did. What are you going to do to me? What punishment can you inflict? Look at me.' She spreads her arms wide as if hiding nothing. 'Look at me, at what I am, what I've seen. How can you punish me further?' She yelps her raw laugh.

Cain blinks. Swallows. Brings his bar stool closer to hers. 'Did you?' he says, speaking low. 'Did you kill him?'

'Now, why would I do that?' asks Layla reasonably. 'Perhaps because I didn't like his face?'

Cain pauses; studies her; considers. Finally, he nods. 'People have killed for less.'

Layla's eyes are hard black pebbles. 'That's very true,' she says.

As he pays the tab and leaves, he catches sight of a black cat, slinking and swishing its tail, in the shadows of the dark corner beyond the bar.

WRITING HOME
by
P.J. Stephenson

I don't find it easy to write - even at the best of times.

My mother hasn't heard from me for weeks; my sister never got a reply to her last letter. What can I say to them beyond the usual trite banalities and the repeated expressions of love and devotion, however sincere?

A breeze ripples the canvas of the tent and the candle flickers at my bedside. I grip my pencil tighter but words won't come. My eyelids droop.

We're close to the road here and the noise makes it hard to sleep. Yet I am so exhausted after all my exertions of the last week that I could drop off at any moment. My mother always said an outdoor life makes for a sound sleeper.

My head nods.

I wake with a start.

Was I dreaming? What's that noise?

I lift my head from the pillow.

Birds are singing.

I can't believe my own ears; all I can hear is birdsong. Everything else is still and calm. It can't be.

Nightingales! I know their song from the woods at home, and it's flowing through the crisp night air: melodious, beautiful, magical. And it's not just a faint sound; it's loud. Five or six birds sing at once close by, and even more are singing in the distance.

I sit up in bed. I went to sleep fully clothed and wrapped in a blanket but I am cold. In the half-light I see the candle has burnt down to a pool of yellowy wax. What a waste. My paper and pencil are caught up in the bedding; I retrieve them and put them in my shirt pocket.

I get up slowly and quietly so as not to wake the others. I slip on my coat and boots, lift the tent flap and step outside.

Moonbeams stream down on our campsite, illuminating the surrounding bushes and trees in a glow that is at once both so natural yet so unnatural. The birds seem to be celebrating this glorious moonlit night; their singing fills the air - a burst of life when I least expected it.

I creep slowly down the path into the woods. As I pass by bushes and thicket the birdsong is louder, building as if to a crescendo, echoing around the small copse of beech, oak and birch. There are several groups of birds singing at once. I've never heard anything like it.

I love nightingales; their song is so varied and melodic. And my spirits rise with every trilling note, every fluted whistle. The music ripples and gurgles through my soul.

The moon casts shadows out of the ancient, gnarled branches; some look eerily like arms reaching for the sky. I shiver and wrap my coat tighter around me.

I stand still and close my eyes, listening.

I dare to take a deep breath through my nose. The cold air fills my nostrils. And with it comes the damp smell of wood and moss and leaf litter.

I am transported back to my childhood, playing in the countryside in rural Oxfordshire. My brother and I used to do so much outdoors: fishing for trout in the crystal clear streams and cooking our catch over an open fire; collecting frog spawn from murky green ponds and watching each day as the semolina-like eggs turned miraculously into tadpoles; and, of course, collecting birds' eggs.

The shame comes back to me as if it were yesterday. I had been so proud of myself at first. My older brother, Matthew, struggled to reach the higher branches of the tree but, slim and lithe and acrobatic, I succeeded where he had failed and I reached the goshawk nest.

I hadn't expected the hen to be there; she must have returned while I was climbing. As I hauled myself up onto the last branch the huge bird of prey let out a loud, piercing screech. I saw its face: its curved yellow beak gaping open, red eyes burning into my skull from under bright white eyebrows. Then I felt the back draft as it thumped into the sky in a wash of feathers.

I was so surprised I nearly lost my grip. But as the bird arched up out of the canopy I managed to steady myself. Taking a deep breath, I leaned into the nest and saw three, bluish-white, two-inch long eggs. I snatched one quickly, put it in my shirt pocket and scrambled back to earth.

I raced my brother home to tell my father of my daring feat. He hunted - crows, rabbits, foxes, pheasants; I knew he'd be happy for me.

He was angry. He told me I probably scared the birds off for good. All the eggs would go cold and the chicks inside would die. Didn't I know that goshawks kept the vermin down? We needed them.

I pleaded my defence: I took only one egg. But I felt ashamed – I hadn't meant to ruin the whole clutch.

I never went egg collecting again.

My father gave me an old pair of army binoculars and I became a birdwatcher instead of a bird killer. I used to love walking in the woods, spotting different species flitting in the canopy or skulking in the undergrowth. Matthew often joined me and we would hide near nests just to watch the parents bring food to their chicks. From chaffinches to woodpeckers, we marvelled at the innate parental instincts of these beautiful creatures, working tirelessly to keep their offspring alive and growing. How could I have ever taken eggs and killed the babies?

A tear rolls down my cheek. It's just the first... Weeks of pent up stress and grief are finally released and I find myself crying out loud, salty drops streaming down my face, moistening and warming my cold cheeks.

I stifle my sobs. I can't disturb the birds. I mustn't disturb the birds. Not again.

I know there is no hope of seeing the nightingales tonight – they are deep in the undergrowth. Like sun coming through clouds on a rainy day, I smile through my torrent of tears as I realize I'm not killing birds now, I'm not even watching them; I'm just listening to them.

And I have never heard anything like it. Usually nightingales sing alone; tonight they have all come together like an avian choir. And what a chorus. It's incredible that such a small, brown, plain-looking bird can produce such beautiful sounds. No wonder Shakespeare waxed lyrically about nightingale song. I want the moment to go on for hours.

Which, of course, it can't.

An ear-splitting blast shatters the peaceful night like a pebble through glass. It is one of our big guns, an eighteen pounder. The earth trembles. The birds fall silent.

Suddenly the smell of death and decay overwhelms the odour of wet logs and leaves. Then the whole battery opens up from alongside the road. Huge shells go whistling over my head through the clear night sky.

I shiver uncontrollably; my whole body shakes. The birdsong has gone. The wood is no longer a place of magic and beauty.

The smell has changed again; I now feel the tingle of cordite in my nostrils. I know it's my imagination - I am too far from the guns. But it is real to me, and it makes me gag.

I need to get away from the shadows and the smells, to find light and warmth. I turn and hurry back to camp, wiping my damp face on the back of my hand.

I am fagged out but don't want to go back into the officers' tent as I know I won't be able to sleep again. Coming out of the woods, I wind my way hastily through the rows of marquees to the edge of camp.

A brazier is roaring, flames licking at the coke, a beacon of hot light in the night. A sentry is standing there, warming his hands. He raises dark, shadowed eyes at my approach, salutes me wearily, then resumes his posture – arms straight out in front of him like a sleep walker.

I put my hands to the fire too and try to chase the chill from my bones; it is so very deep in my bones. I never used to shake with cold yet I shiver so often these days.

The flames crackle. We don't speak. We don't move. All our concentration is focused on being as relaxed and as warm as possible, and trying to shut out the noise of the guns.

After a few minutes, the sentry stirs and shifts his rifle to the other shoulder.

"Tea'll be along soon, sir," he says, as much to comfort himself as to announce the impending breakfast to me. "It's good 'ere. Do you remember that place where it always tasted of petrol?"

It's a rhetorical question. We all remember.

As my hands begin to warm up and steam starts to rise from the arms of my eternally damp coat, I stop shaking. I sit down on a log and take out my pencil and paper. In the light of the fire I finally scratch the words that have been so difficult to find.

A British Army Camp
France
30 April 1918.

Dear Mother,
    I heard the most amazing sound tonight.
    You know how much I like bird watching. I haven't seen a bird since I can remember. That's hardly surprising: in the Somme and at Ypres there were no trees – all I ever saw were blackened, charred stumps. But here, in the part of France where I find myself now, there are proper hedges and woods, not yet destroyed by artillery.
    My company and I are in reserve, a few miles back from the front line. Our gunners have been giving the German trenches a serious pounding and it's been hard to sleep. It must be even harder for Fritz. The Huns are getting a dose of it tonight and must be in for a fairly thin time. Nothing less than they deserve, of course.
    But tonight, for five minutes, our guns stopped. And, in that pause, in that small chink of peace, nature tried to claim back this little area of forgotten countryside.
    Nightingales sang! I couldn't believe it.
    It made me think immediately of Matthew – he'd have loved it. It even got me thinking of our egg collecting days.
    I miss him so much – I'm sure you do too. I can't believe he's gone. I met one of the officers from his regiment recently. He confirmed Matthew wouldn't

have felt a thing. The trench mortar landed right in the
middle of his machine gun nest.

I was remembering...

"Writing home, sir?"

I look up at the sentry and nod.

"I envy you," he says. "I never know what to write. I 'ave a dickens of a time of it. How do you explain to someone back in England what we've been through and the life we lead? I mean, where do you start, sir?" He gazes wistfully into the fire.

"It's hard," I say, though whether I'm referring to letter writing or the life we lead, I am not sure.

And as the guns pound, and the heavy shells go whistling through the air, I write to my mother.

THE LAST VOYAGE OF FERRYWOMAN KATHERINE MARSHALL

by

John Bunting

Her first thought as she stirred from stasis-sleep was, "Made it! Now for a quiet retirement in the desert." Her second thought was, "What the hell is all that noise!" Her third thought was, "Oh bugger, alarm bells!" She gasped as the starship's emergency revival system pressed an oxygen mask hard to her face, then wretched violently as it pulled the bio-analysis tube from her throat. Finally, as the stasis-bed lifted her into a sitting position, she vomited through the mask and all over her trousers. Ferrywoman Katherine Marshall was awake.

She dragged off the puke filled mask, and wiped her face with her shirt. "Computer," she screamed above the bedlam, "why all the alarms? Report."

"My mother told me never to talk to strange women."

"What?! Damn it, computer, it's me. Stop being bloody stupid!"

"Only following procedure; hint hint."

Katherine groaned in frustration, and eased herself off the bed. Two deep breaths, and she started towards the door, only to find herself flat on her nose as her legs refused to cooperate. Cursing loudly, she heaved herself up onto all fours, and scrambled on. She entered the Bridge on hands and knees, hauled herself up onto her Captain's chair, and pushed her hand into the DNA Analyser. "Computer, Waking Procedure Calamity; recognise Ferrywoman Marshall, Katherine Anabella, service number five one two, authorisation code Captain Alpha Female Definitely Most Definitely Bloody Female Alpha."

"Ferrywoman Marshall is recognised."

"About time. Turn off that noise! Thankyou. And the flashing lights. Now; report why."

"Report why what, Maam?"

"What! What do you mean why what? Why was every effing alarm on the ship going off? That's why what."

"Maam, twenty-two seconds ago, I detected a large unidentifiable vessel seven million miles away heading straight for us. I altered our course to avoid it, only to note with considerable consternation that one-hundredth of a second later the vessel armed its *very* big guns, and changed its course too. So I initiated your emergency waking procedure, and sounded the collision alarm. I then checked our defensive and offensive weapons systems, only to find with equal consternation that both are inoperable. So I sounded the action stations alarm. For reasons I will explain later, but to do with the fact that sixty-three percent of my other systems are down as well, I sounded the general alarm – just so as you'd know we have a number of issues to deal with. I await your instructions."

"…Pardon?"

"Maam, twenty-two—"

"Stop; I get it. When will it reach us?"

"In eight minutes."

"Have you tried all the emergency collision manoeuvres?"

"Yes."

"There's nothing we can do to avoid it?"

"No."

"And it's got very big guns?"

"Maam, it's got very bigger, faster, everythinger than us; and it's coming our way."

"There must be something. You're always bragging you have an IQ of two hundred."

"Nothing."

Katherine sat thinking for a while, then said quietly, "So you're telling me we might be going to die. I must say, this is all very sudden."

"Technically, I won't die, I'll break up into several million pieces. But both your observations are valid."

"Well, it was always a risk of the job I guess." Katherine sniffed at her stinking clothes. "But I certainly don't want to meet my maker smelling like this." She walk/crawled over to the shower room, washed herself down, and put on her best uniform. Then she stretched and eased her muscles loose. Feeling better, she went and stood by the computer. "I'm sorry it's ending this way," she sighed. "What is it; fourteen trips together?"

"It is. We've had some laughs, haven't we? Do you remember… no… best not to start that."

"No. As a matter of interest, where are we?"

"I have no idea."

"Huh?"

"Maam, when our ship arrived at where I thought Earth was, it… um… wasn't. Nor were any of the other planets or the sun. The whole bloody solar system had disappeared. I wondered if the problem might rest with me, so I carried out a wide-ranging test of my navigation system. It turned out I was A.OK. As a result, I concluded that we had been on course – it was the Earth that hadn't been."

"When was this?"

"Seven thousand four hundred and two Earth years ago. Give or take."

"Seven… and you didn't think to wake me?"

"There didn't seem much point. If I didn't know where Earth was you sure as hell wouldn't, and you'd have blundered around the Bridge getting cross with me, and using up valuable and diminishing consumables."

"Blundered arou… Computer, if I may say so, you seem to have developed a rather eccentric way of addressing your Captain."

"Sorry, Maam. All those extra years of background radiation have not treated my linguistic circuits well. Nor any of my others; hence many of them being down. The foul expletives are your fault."

"So you've never found Earth?"

"Nope."

"Shit."

"Indeed."

They fell silent; both, in their different ways, contemplating the apparently inevitable. Katherine thought about the life she had chosen as a Ferrywoman. On the whole she'd enjoyed it. One month loading; two hundred years in stasis-sleep, only to be woken in extreme emergency; and one month unloading. And then a year off before the return trip. It was during one of those rest years that she'd fallen in love with the empty hotness of the Central European Desert. "It is, isn't it," she muttered to herself.

"What is what, Maam?"

"Mmm? Oh, I was thinking how ironic it is that my last ferry trip – in fact, the last ever sub-light ferry trip by anyone if they've got that faster-than-light drive to work – proves to be the only one ever lost."

"Irony is… whoa, hang on, Maam. Hang on one little-bitty minute; the unidentifiable vessel has started to slow. On current projections, it should stop one mile off our port bow in… ten seconds. And it's switched off its guns! Yippee, we're not going to die; not yet anyway."

"On screen." The vessel was a mass of white cubes and globes, joined together by an intricate maze of thick, tube-like structures. And it was huge; maybe ten miles in every direction.

"There's an audio message coming through."

"Let's hear it."

"Identify yourself," rasped a deep voice.

"Bloody hell," gasped Katherine, "it's talking in English!"

"Never mind that; identify yourself immediately!"

"I am Ferrywoman Katherine Marshall, Captain of the star-ferry Godstone. I am on a peaceful mission carrying non-military supplies from the planet Oxted, in the gamma quadrant, to my home planet Earth. I mean you no harm."

"Wait while we interrogate your ship's computer."

"Ouch, that hurts!"

It's OK, computer, let them do it. We need their help."

"You speak the truth. I am Becklespinax the Ninety-Second, Captain of the Saurship Goyocephale Three. I am opening a visual channel; I think you will find what you see will be of interest."

"OMG!"

"What is *that*?"

"A dinosaur."

"Correct."

"Hey, my first alien. What a cracker!"

"I and my kind are the descendants of the First Magyarosaurus Solar Expeditionary Squadron, which had the good fortune to be in transit when that wretched meteor struck Earth, our home planet also, and killed off everysaur. How their deep space radar missed the damn thing I'll never know. Anyway, the Squadron managed to land on an habitable planet in the beta quadrant, and the rest, as you would say, is history. You are in considerable trouble, are you not?"

"You're not kidding."

"We seem to have lost Earth."

"That's because it's disappeared."

"…Continue."

"Yes! I've always wanted you to say that."

"We've no idea where to. We've been monitoring Earth's progress for several million years, and what we do know is that a while back this area of the galaxy drifted into psychedelic space, and lots of star systems simply vanished, including yours."

"What space?"

"These parts of the space/time continuum were damaged when some mindless idiot tested a faster-than-light drive. The effect on the continuum of the impossible actually happening was similar to that on your brain if you took Lysergic Diethylamide."

"LSD?"

"No shit. Warped space!"

"Your ship entered the psychedelic space when it approached where Earth should have been. You're trapped."

"Are you… trapped?"

No. Our scientists have developed a mobile force field that can keep out psychedelic space by generating an artificial normal space around us."

"Wow; that is genuinely cool, and very, very clever. Respect to the dinosaurs."

"It's only a temporary fix. Psychedelic space is unstable and collapsing at an increasing rate. It will shortly fall into a massive black hole. We need to leave soon or we never will. And here's the thing; we've been trying unsuccessfully to rescue you for a while now."

"I don't remember any previous attempts."

"You're stuck in a time loop; each time we meet is like the first for you. That's why I've treated this meeting as a First Contact, and interrogated your systems as you would expect me to. But this must be our last attempt."

"What do you suggest?"

"Our scientists have tried every sensible idea they can think of, without success, so as a last resort we're going to try something completely crazy. LSD crazy, hopefully. Computer, what are you carrying in your cargo hold?"

"Nine hundred and eighty-two million genetically identical, butter-basted, oven-ready, frozen chickens."

"Is that animal, vegetable or mineral?"

"Good question. They contain various disgusting vegetable and mineral additives, and far too much water in my opinion, but on the whole I would say animal."

"Can you release them into space?"

"That's up to my Captain."

"Could we detach the cargo hold, and then blow a hole in it?"

"Yes, but as the man said, you're only supposed to blow the bloody—"

"Enough! And the sudden decompression should blast the hold apart?"

"Confirmed."

"We'll do that, then. Computer, make it so."

"Compliance."

"It will be sufficient."

"And then?"

"And then watch and hope. If our plan works, it will force space/time back into normality, Earth will reappear where it was, and you will wake up safe in its orbit as if none of this had happened... which... err, it won't have."

"And I can retire to the Central Earth Desert. Sounds good to me."

"But if it doesn't work, you will wake up in the middle of a collapsing black hole, which... won't be good. We have two of your minutes left; we must act now."

Katherine took a deep breath. "What are our chances?"

"Better than zero, which is what they will be if we don't do this."

"Fair point. Thank you for putting yourselves at risk for us."

"Here jolly here. You dinosaurs rock. Maybe see you on the other side!"

Katherine pressed an emergency release button, and the cargo hold drifted away for the ferry-ship. At a safe distance, she pressed another button, and the hold blew apart. Out exploded nine hundred and eighty-two million frozen chickens. Immediately, the Saurship bathed them in an orange glow of microwaves, and the chickens thawed. Exposed to the effects of psychedelic space, they started to change colour and shape, and within a few seconds nine hundred and eighty-two million pink flying pigs were grunting and flapping around helplessly. Now a green energy beam fired from the Saurship, and the pink flying pigs were somehow twisted and faded into the very fabric of the space/time continuum, which seemed to shiver as one psychedelic distortion was confronted by another. The third-to-last thing Katherine heard was herself whispering, "Our father..." The second-to-last thing she heard was, *"Goodbye Ferrywoman Katherine Marshall, and good luck."* The last thing she heard was, **"Holy shit, I hope the force is with us. Continue. Hah."**

Katherine's first thought as she stirred from stasis-sleep was...

THIS YEAR, NEXT YEAR, SOMETIME, NEVER

by

Taria Karillion

I cried all night.

I've known Eddie from next door my whole life and Mother says we've been inseparable for most of it. Our mums had us on the same day in the same hospital and we were best friends for years before we fell in love. My folks love him, his love me. It was just meant to be.

So it was The Biggest Shock Ever when Dad said no.

Our palms had stuck to each other's with sweat outside Dad's study. I'd mouthed an 'ow' at his pale smile as his big, strong hand squeezed mine. Just like my sister's boyfriend had, Eddie had slunk in, his dark eyes bigger than a bush baby's. I'd pressed my ear hard to the door, the *throb-a-throb-a-throb* against the wood like the clock on a quiz show.

When he came out, Eddie looked more stunned and distraught than the day Rex ate his Teddy Ruxpin when we were three.

Maybe it was too soon after my sister's 'arm-and-a-leg' wedding. I offered my entire savings, but Dad just looked over his half-moon glasses at me and gave this odd sort of laugh. He actually *laughed*! That was cruel. I'd not seen Dad be cruel before. I didn't know what to say - I just cried.

We asked Mum to speak to him, but she just shook her head, hugged us and welled up. We spoke to Eddie's parents, but they said it simply couldn't be allowed, but didn't explain why.

We talked about eloping, going to the Registry office and emigrating like Nana had, but Eddie said that as an only child he couldn't do that – who would look after his Mum and Dad now they were old?

I began to get suspicious. Maybe there was something about Eddie that no-one was telling me.

My mother's job at the hospital library could be the answer. So the next time I was there, I tried to sneak a look at the patient records computer. Very naughty, I know, but someone had left it logged in. I'd entered our date of birth when Mum's old biddy boss walked in. That was tooooo close – and my quickest screen change to Solitaire ever.

How else could I get an answer? In the end I decided to ask Dad straight up. Why? Why shouldn't Eddie and I get married? I couldn't understand why he'd refused to give his blessing!

I stayed calm. I didn't raise my voice. I was respectful, but insistent. I demanded to know exactly what the reason was. And he looked me in the eye, steadily, with no laughter this time, and he told me.

"My sweet girl – and you will *always* be my little girl, no matter how old you are - the simple truth is this... It's impossible for you and Edward to get married – it just isn't allowed..."

I couldn't stop my lip from wobbling as he continued,

"...not when you're only seven years old."

BLACKCURRANT JELLY
by
Rhodri Diaz

It's the sky that gets you. Everything else, you get used to. Bare-boned buildings, gutted and decaying. The pervasive smell; sulphur tinged with rotting carcass. After a while, it all feels normal. But the sky, a sky the colour of blackcurrant jelly, that's something you never quite adjust to. Sometimes, you wake up and it'll be paler, more diluted. Then you start to think, to wish, that maybe the universe is correcting itself. That maybe things will go back to the way they were before. Hope is our only currency, and we're running dangerously short.

The rotting, the madness, the world crumbling around us, all of that happened slowly, methodically. We had time to adjust our eyes to the new light. But the jelly sky, that hit immediately. Something comfortable, something familiar, was forcibly taken from us. We went to sleep in our own bed and woke up in a strange one. It didn't take us long to realise that we will never sleep comfortably again.

He hates it when I talk about before. He says that nostalgia isn't productive. That the future is what counts. I'm not sure that there is a future. But I can't tell him that. I need him. I need something to hold on to. We all do in this world. I wish I could have loved him before all this. Before everything was finished.

He'll wake up soon. I don't want to see his face when he looks outside. You forget while you're asleep. The best part of the day is when you wake up and, for the briefest of blissful seconds, still think you're dreaming. That moment is what we live for.

We still have coffee. That freeze dried stuff lasts forever. I miss milk though. It's strange, the little things you never realise you'll miss until they're taken from you. Milk, chocolate, the BBC. They feel like relics from an ancient, unknowable world.

I bring the coffee to the cracked glass table beside him. He stirs and rubs the gritty sleep out of his eyes. He fell asleep on the sofa last night. Fatigue is a common side effect. The roots of his hair are turning a mossy colour. Scaly red patches cover his body. His forehead burns like a furnace. A week together. A week of normality. That's all I want.

I was the one that pulled him out of the wreckage. I got on my hands and knees and I dug until my hands bled. I don't know why I chose him. Why I chose that building. There were others in need. Others that died because no one stepped in. I wish I could say that it wasn't because he was beautiful, but I think it was. Love was the only thing that was still in our control. I needed him or I would have been lost.

He smiles when he wakes up and looks over at me. We do this every morning. I wake up, make coffee, he smiles at me. The biggest smile he can muster. It makes us feel normal. It's kept me alive. I store it away, for future reference.

He takes a tentative sip. I apologise for the bitterness. We lost sugar a long time ago. He chuckles, like it's the most trivial thing in the world and we can just get some later from the corner shop. I don't know where he gets it from, that boundless optimism. "One day, we'll have sugar." he says.

It only takes a minute before he's rushing to the bathroom. The coffee hasn't been staying down long lately. There are red flecks on the sink bowl. One more day, if we're lucky.

I know what has to be done. I know it but I don't want to believe it. We all think that we could do it. With our backs against the wall, when nothing else was possible. But when it comes to it, looking at him hunched over the sink bowl bringing up that bitter freeze dried crap, I'm not sure I have it in me. But it has to be done. For his sake. What was that phrase in the old days? 'Cruel to be kind'.

He spies me out of the corner of his eye and tries to wash away any evidence before I can see it. He laughs again. It's an unsure laugh, as if he expects me to validate him. I'm not sure I have any laughs left in me. But I validate him, all the same.

I sit on the lid of the toilet seat and I think about love. I often used to do this, before, with some miserable pop band playing and the memory of an ill-fated tryst swirling around in my head. I used to think that love was the willingness to do the littlest things for someone and, at the same time, the biggest things. Back then, love was a mess of contradictions. It made you want to run forward, run towards something brighter, more exciting and at the same time, it made you want to run backwards, towards something safer. I'm too scared of going forward. All I want to do is run back towards something that made some sense. Now I know that love is complete dependence, a tie that binds you to another person. And the bitter truth of it is that the only people who survive in our world are people without ties, and the people who manage to stay sane long enough to survive are those with ties. Rock and a hard place.

He's on the rat-bitten couch when I come out, flicking through some tatty paperback, the only one that survived, some sensationalist piece of garbage they used to churn out by the thousands. He hates it too, you can see by the way his nose crinkles when he reads a particularly lurid paragraph. I imagine what his taste would have been. Woolf, definitely Woolf. Edith Wharton. The Beats. God, he'd have been perfect. We could have sat around all day, discussing aestheticism in Wilde or first-wave feminism, then we'd make love and go to bed. Rinse and repeat until we're old and withered, sitting in adjacent chairs in some far-flung nursing home, stinking of stale piss and Fisherman's Friends.

We live, we exist, opposite what was once the university, my university. It was the pride and joy of our city, towering Victorian architecture, red brick and just ostentatious enough that everyone knew what kind of serious learning went on there. Now it's a shell, still burning inside, red brick turned ash. If you look closely, you'll sometimes see a scrap of paper from a book or a journal, a couple of words still legible in amongst the debris. A message from the time before. If you look even closer, you'll see knobs of bone and clumps of hair. No one looks that close.

I imagine seeing him, lounging on the long stretch of field in front of the main hall. It'd be a sweltering day, the kind of day where even the buildings and the trees seem to sweat. Absent-mindedly, he'd finger through a dog-eared old book of heady, flowery poetry. Lost to the world, caught up in cadence and wordplay. I'd imagine a thousand different conversation starters. I'd say I'd read that particular book of poetry, though I hadn't, and loved it entirely. He'd catch me out somehow, quote me a passage that doesn't appear and I'd nod and gush about Keats or Rimbaud and he'd laugh at my foolishness,. I'd see the dewy perspiration on his brow and I'd imagine making love to him. He'd move closer to me, tastefully, and we'd share the poetry. I'd notice how he smelled, sandalwood and the suggestion of sweat. After an hour or two, he'd have a lecture to attend. He'd promise that we'd meet again. I almost believe this really happened.

I excuse myself and slip into the bedroom. The bed is unmade, a tangled ball of filthy damp-smelling sheets. For a while, we were regimental about changing the bed. It was ritual, a slice of normal life. Now, it feels like time that no one has to waste. Sitting gingerly on the edge of the bed, I pry open the bottom drawer of the side table. In among the passports, birth certificates, family photo albums, the detritus of ancient life, I catch a glimpse of dull grey metal. Puffing out my cheeks, I pick it up carefully. I've inspected every inch of this pistol over the last few weeks. Checked the ammo a thousand times. Two rounds.

The first night we were together, we made love. He was still tender from his injuries. But he asked me, he begged me. He needed to feel close to someone. Afterwards, we lay in bed and we held each other and wept. It seemed strange, that everything had crumbled but sex was still there, still the same. No matter what, they couldn't take that away from us. Sex was our weapon, our way of rebelling, against God, against fate, against whatever had done this to us.

When I come out of the bedroom, he's napping on the couch, the lurid book still open on his chest. You try and sleep as much as you can. Forget as much as you can. There's a spot of red on his chin. He'd saved the worst for when I'd left. I look at the hunk of metal in my hand. The cannonball in my stomach is trying to make a grand exit. I hope my retch doesn't wake him. Red flecks on the sink bowl. It's happening to me too.

I check the ammo again. It's enough. I snap it shut and steel myself. I'm doing this for him. He opens his eyes slowly. He asks if I'm okay, but he soon catches a glimpse of what's in my hand. It's unbearable. His eyes fix on me. I can see every little change of emotion, every tiny register, from fear to anger to understanding to regret. He pleads with me, without saying anything, not a single word. He wonders if there's anything else we could do. We could get medicine, or see if we could find other survivors who could help. No, he knows as well as I do. They'd shoot us on sight. This is the only way.

I sit next to him on the couch. Tears slide down his cheeks. I can't look at anything but the roots of his hair. I kiss him, tasting the tang of iron on his lips. He smells like sandalwood. I pull the gun up to the side of his head and with one last embrace and "I love you" on my tongue, I release him. He goes limp in my arms. I let his head loll backwards and pull the hair from his face. He's smiling. I've done the right thing.

My hand is shaking violently as I put the barrel to my own temple. I can't feel anything below the waist. I wonder how it came to this, how everything decayed underneath us. I think of the day when I pulled him from the wreckage and I remember hoping that maybe now everything would be okay, that maybe together we could take on the world. I pray, for the first time in years, to someone I know isn't there. I think of him on the lawn of the university and I think of how our lives would have gone. I imagine a passionate summer affair and a cool autumn romance and I imagine how we would have grown old together and for a moment, just before the darkness, I'm happy.

SITTING PRETTY

by

Craig McEwan

I was happily lost in the streets of nineteen-fifties New York, when a sharp voice dragged me from the pages of my book.

'Hello? Mind if I join you?' it said—or repeated—judging by its tone. I kept my gaze lowered. 'May I sit here? *Please*?'

The crowded hospital canteen was heavy with the rumble of conversation; I flapped a hand in apology.

'Hey, I'm just gonna pull on in, and if that bothers you, speak up, okay?'

The girl's left foot was in a cast, covered with a purple stocking. Her straw-straight hair was pillar-box red, and she had as many rings in her ears as on her fingers. She was roughly my age, almost fifteen, though I must have looked ancient next to her, in my cords and polo shirt.

She must have cool parents, I thought. *Mine would have chickens if I so much as spiked up my hair.* With a nudge at her joystick, she moved her wheelchair closer, took a pack of sandwiches, crisps and an apple from the basket on the handlebars, and set them out on the table. *My* table. Her clothes, like her lipstick, and the stormy sky outside, were coal black.

She was fabulous.

'What you reading?' She reached over, right into my personal space, and tipped back my book. 'Catcher in the Rye. You've got taste, or your teacher has.'

I stole a glance at her chair. Like mine, it wasn't the sort you get issued with for a temporary incapacity like a broken foot. Motorised and personalised, with a cup holder and faded stickers on the back panel. Too small for her: she'd be due an upgrade soon, if her parents could afford it or were industrious fundraisers.

'I'd rather read Iain Banks.' I said.

'Oh yeah, The Wasp Factory! That book is awesome!'

'I prefer his sci-fi.' *Knucklehead!*

'Oh.'

'The Wasp Factory's great too.' Despite myself I was getting drawn into conversation. Imagine if... but who was I trying to kid? This cool, confident, gorgeous girl would never be interested in a geek like me. No one would, except for a couple of the most idiotic girls at school, and who needs them? Girls are more Toby's field. My clever, kind, handsome, funny brother. I love him, but I also hate him. I wish he'd never been born sometimes, or that I hadn't.

'Have you read *Carrie*?' I asked.

'Stephen King? Not yet,' she said. 'Mum says I can watch the film when I'm sixteen. I heard it's fantastic.'

I twisted my brain trying to think of something to say that wouldn't make me sound like a jerk. I don't talk to girls that often, especially not ball-achingly cool and beautiful girls who read good books, and wear clothes that would give my mum a seizure.

'What's your name?' she asked. I wish I'd thought of that.

'Ben.'

There was a pause of around two weeks as I mentally tried out and discarded about a thousand potential topics of conversation. A dimple appeared in her ghost-like cheek, and she extended her hand.

'Ellie.' She was laughing, but it was kind, not a hateful and cruel laugh; not the sort you get from one of Naomi Wood's gang at school. Her palm was cool and dry as it touched mine. I could feel my heartbeat in my hair.

Luckily, Ellie is far less dumb than me, and from that point on, the conversation flowed like Niagara. We had loads in common, and she was much, much nicer than you'd expect from her hair and clothes. We were both sputtering giggles at something witty I'd said, or she'd said, when I noticed that both her arms, but especially the left, carried a fine tracery of white scars, barely visible beneath her bracelets. I tried not to, but Ellie caught me staring.

'I cut myself sometimes. Is that alright with you?' she said, thrusting her chin forward.

'It's your body,' I said.

I shifted my chair to get more legroom, but Ellie said, 'Oh, right—roll away. Who are you to judge me?'

'I'm not judging. But your mum and dad—'

'Mum, you mean. Not everyone has two parents you know, Mister Perfect-Family.'

'Your mum, then, must have enough to worry about without making it worse by...' I gestured weakly at her arms, my words letting me down as usual.

'I've stopped doing it now anyway, for the exact reasons you're too tongue-tied to—'

'Eleanor Louise Rouse!' A puce-faced woman was marching towards us. 'Get out of that wheelchair this instant!'

The woman's knuckles were white on the handles of a crappy hospital-standard wheelchair. The girl in the chair was contorted with palsy; one hand waved uselessly in the air, her stick-thin legs pushed over to one side. A few years younger than Ellie: about the right size for the wheelchair... the wheelchair that Ellie was miraculously jumping out of, looking toxic with guilt. The room spun a hundred and eighty degrees on its axis. The girls exchanged venomous stares as the woman kept shouting.

'How do you think Sorrel felt when she came out to find her wheelchair gone—stolen!—after her physio appointment?'

Ellie wasn't cool now; she looked like a little girl caught wearing Mummy's make-up.

'Speak up girl! Stop staring at the floor!'

'I was just sitting. I *have* broken my foot.'

'Just sitting—in someone else's wheelchair? Does this lad think you're disabled?'

I had to speak up, but my voice stalled. Again. I sat gawping as the argument continued.

'I didn't tell him anything. We were only talking! Why is everything about Sorrel? All the time, "Sorrel needs this, Sorrel needs that," appointments, groups, "no money for school trips, we spent it on Sorrel," and for once...' The fight left her, and with tears stretching black ropes of make-up down to her jaw she said, quietly '... for once *I* sat in the chair. And people were kind to me. And a lady carried my tray for me. And I met a nice boy and—and people noticed me.'

Inside, I was screaming like a drill sergeant *Me too! We're exactly the same!* But nobody heard: it was just in my head.

'I'm not...' I began, but Ellie silenced me with a glare. A set of keys dangled from her mother's outstretched hand.

'Wait in the car. Try not to steal it.'

I wished, I wished more than anything in the world, that I hadn't been sitting in that chair; that I'd met Ellie on an ordinary day, when I was just being me.

She grabbed the keys and hobbled toward the stairs that led up to ground level. Was that pity on her mum's face, as she gazed down at me? Undeserved pity for a lying, spineless coward?

Was I really going to let this glorious, funny, unstable girl walk out of my life, furious and frustrated? I thought of Naomi Wood and her friends; Ellie would tear them apart, with their pathetic gossip and ill-informed opinions.

I had to move. Now. With a shrug of apology towards Sorrel, I leapt out of Toby's wheelchair.

And ran.

Pushing past the overweight dawdlers blocking the stairway, I took two steps at a time to the top. She couldn't have got far, not in that cast.

I sprinted outside into the daylight, but she was nowhere in sight. I was about to ask the smokers lined up in their hospital beds if they'd seen a beautiful goth girl limp past, when I heard my name. I whirled round, and there she stood, watching me. Laughing in that way she has. A shaft of sunlight pierced the smoke and reflected off someone's drip-stand.

A COVERSATION WITH DEATH
by
Annabel Ashalley-Anthony

Alyssa's eyes fluttered closed, she couldn't take the arguments anymore, she just wanted to sleep, was that so difficult for them to understand?

A warm hand on her shoulder had her eyes opening again.

"It's you," she said smiling.

A nod of a dark head, shrouded in darkness his features weren't easy to distinguish, but she knew this man, trusted him with her life, which was ironic really, considering who he was.

"You are still decided then." It was a question, but like everything he said it sounded like a statement, an absolute truth.

Alyssa sat up and nodded eagerly, the people around her bed ignorant of her actions, still arguing and reasoning amongst themselves, over her. Her opinion wasn't sought, it didn't matter to them what she thought.

"Please," Alyssa begged.

A slow shake of his head, sending his dark hood shifting slightly, even though the room was brightly lit, he stood in darkness, it clung to him like the robes he was wearing.

"Why do you dress like that still? I'm not afraid of you." Alyssa said tilting her head to the side.

She had seen him wear casual clothes, but he was back to his robes again as though he wanted to remind her who he was.

"But you should be," he said quietly.

"I'm not, I'm ready –"

"You are not, you think you are, but you are not. You are too young to understand that; there are things you have not even realised you will miss." He said.

Alyssa just stared at him her face stubborn.

He held out his hand.

"Come with me," he said.

Alyssa eagerly complied; stepping out of her body came naturally to her now, like it no longer belonged to her. She looked down at the stranger, hooked up to the life support machines, surrounded by her family and the best Doctors and Nurses she had ever known, but still it was easy to step away and leave them all. It was far easier for her to take his hand.

He took her to a house she knew too well, a bedroom she hadn't seen for almost a year. It hadn't changed; a picture that her sister had brought to the hospital was still here, on the bookshelf where it belonged. Her bed never as neat as her sister's housed her teddy bears forever waiting for her return.

"Why have you brought me here?" She asked him a catch in her throat as she slowly touched the light pink walls, she remembered having an argument with her sister over the choice, they had settled on painting one side of their room yellow and the other side pink.

"I want to show you, all you will leave behind."

Alyssa gasped as her sister stepped into the room. She looked happier than Alyssa had seen her in a long time. At twelve Penelope was two years older and being tall always looked more mature. Alyssa took a step back as she, or rather a projection of her walked into the room. It was strange seeing herself so vibrant and full of life. Alyssa's projection and Penelope's began painting their nails.

Alyssa's eyes shimmered as she looked away at the scene; so normal and yet something she had been longing for.

The scene shifted, Penelope's and Alyssa's projections were older – in their teens. They were chatting excitedly as they made their way downstairs. Alyssa followed the duo as the doorbell rang. The house was different, the pictures on the wall depicting the passage of a life she couldn't know. She stopped short at the sight of her parents, they looked exactly the same, except Dad's hair was greyer. Mum whispered something in Dad's ear a smile on her lips as Dad narrowed his eyes at a boy who looked to be sixteen; he was shifting from one foot to the other.

Alyssa glanced at her companion.

"The first boy you ever love." He explained.

The scene shifted again and she was graduating, she looked so different, the hair she had always struggled to grow, had been cut very short almost pixie, but it suited her older face; she'd even pierced the top of her ear. The older version of her smiled as she went to hug her sister and her parents who were applauding and beaming at her.

Alyssa blinked rapidly.

"I don't want to see anymore." Alyssa said but the tears wouldn't stop as she kept wiping her face over and over again.

"One more." He said.

The scene shifted and it was her and her sister's bedroom again, except everything was different, the walls were painted a dark plum and a deep blue, even as they grew older they would always disagree on the colours. The shelves were empty; boxes spewed around everywhere as though they were moving. An older version of both of them lay on separate beds but they had both closed the divide by reaching out their hands to each other.

"Ally?" Penelope said softly.

"Yeah?" Alyssa's projection said.

"Even if we are miles apart, promise me that we will always find our way back to each other?" Penelope asked.

"Always," Alyssa's projection responded.

The scene shifted and she was standing in the bedroom again, the one she had left behind.

"Why are you doing this?" She asked.

"You are too young to die." He responded.

"You have taken younger, why are you hesitating?" She asked.

"Because you have a choice to live, take it." It was as close to a plea she had ever heard him make.

Alyssa shook her head.

"Let me show you something." She reached out for his hand, "take me back."

Suddenly they were back at the hospital again and her broken body was before them, her parents were still arguing with the doctors and Penelope was sat in the corner, doing her homework, but every so often she would look up, tears shining in her eyes.

"Listen to them," Alyssa said softly.

"I know what I said, but I can't bear to give up on her. I want to keep her on life support for as long as possible!" Mum said angrily.

The Doctor sighed.

"That's fine Marianne, it really is, but Ally will still be in pain, we are talking about multiple organ failure, she'll be in constant pain until the end. If she doesn't want to prolong things –"

"She's ten for Christ sakes! What does she know about a decision like this?!" Mum said.

"We will not take any action without your consent, but –"

"You're damn right you won't!" Mum said and she glared at Dad who hadn't yet spoken.

"We won't, but," Doctor Anthony said slowly, "please re-consider, think about it from her point of view –"

"I am, and she is a child!"

"For a child to even be considering this option, says something about her mind-set, she's spoken with the therapist –"

"I don't care whose she's spoken with, who in their right mind would sign-off a child on their decision to die?" Mum said glaring at Dr Asante, the therapist, in disgust.

"We don't want to upset you anymore," Doctor Anthony said placidly and she and the other Doctors left the room.

Mum burst into tears as she turned to Dad, and Alyssa watched them with a lump in her throat and a heavy feeling in her chest. She looked up, but her companion was staring at her parents with a sad look in his eyes.

"See how much pain I cause them, and I'll only cause them more and more, even after I'm gone I'll cause them pain, so why should I prolong things any more than I have to? Every day I will be in pain, and they'll be miserable watching me in pain. I can put an end to this right now, right here, I can choose, I can die and set them free."

"You are too young, to speak so easily of death." He said turning to her.

"I wouldn't speak to death if death didn't speak back." She said.

She could already feel the pull of her body again; she had been away from it for too long.

"Think about it," she asked him, as she slipped once more into her body.

"I will if you will." He said before he vanished.

The monitors began beeping as soon as Alyssa fully merged with her body. She didn't know how she could forget this level of pain, she gasped for breath even as the tubes fed her oxygen, was in agony even though the medicine numbed out her body.

She felt pressure on both her hands and she slowly opened her eyes, it was funny how much such a small movement cost her, when she had walked and talked so easily in spirit form.

"Penny?" She asked softly, her vocal cords raw and rough from abuse and disuse.

"I'm here," Penelope said from the foot of her bed, she was blinking rapidly and Alyssa felt herself beginning to cry before she stopped herself.

"Mum,"

More pressure on her left hand.

"I'm here baby, I'm here," Mum said, her voice thick with emotion.

"Dad?" Alyssa tried to turn her head, but the movement was too painful and she stopped as she felt a tear slip down her face.

"Shh, don't move Ally, I'm here." Dad said softly kissing her right hand and he pressed something on the machine so it would give her another dose of medication.

"Please, please, I can't do this anymore," she paused as she took in a ragged breath, "you have to let me go, please let me go." She pleaded, and she felt the tears rolling down her face.

"Don't ask that of us Ally, you don't know what you are saying." Mum said crying.

Alyssa looked at Dad, after weeks of asking, they had both agreed with her yesterday.

"How can I let you go?" He asked, tears in his eyes.

"I understand," Penelope said slowly, "I don't accept it, but I understand." She wiped furiously at her face.

Mum began to cry harder.

"You have to fight Ally, you have to fight this." Dad said squeezing her hand a little harder.

"I have, and I'm tired, so tired. Please, I don't want to fight anymore, I just want to rest." Alyssa said slowly, her speech was slurred as she felt the effects of the increased dose.

"We want more time." Dad said.

Alyssa tried to shake her head but her eyes were closing as the medicine overtook her compulsion to stay awake.

*

Alyssa came awake slowly to the sound of hushed but urgent voices.

"Just let me hold her in peace." Mum said.

"I can't watch her dying before she actually dies." Dad said sadly.

Alyssa tried to open her eyes to tell them to stop.

"She's only a child, she…she can survive." Mum said desperately.

"Stop this, she's dying and," Dad cleared his throat, "she wants to die, and as hard as it is for me to even consider, I have to let her go."

"No, no, I need more time." Mum said.

"We always knew we were living on borrowed time, ten years, the Doctors didn't think we'd even have one. Her sickle cell has ravaged her enough, we were only borrowing her from heaven, but we have to give her back." Dad said.

Alyssa felt herself drift into unconsciousness.

Alyssa woke up again, she felt oddly peaceful as she opened her eyes and saw the dark figure at the door.

"You've come for me?" She asked hopefully.

A slow nod.

"Say goodbye." He said softly.

"I love you and thank you," she said looking at Mum, Dad, the doctors and nurses then finally at Penelope.

There were tears everywhere.

Alyssa smiled as she felt her eyes flutter close.

TILL DEATH US DO PART

by

Maggie Davies

I put my arms around Neil and kissed the top of his head. His hair might be the colour of fresh snow but he was far from an old man. 'We could die together,' I said. 'Fly to Switzerland. Make a holiday out of it. Then finish up at that special clinic they've got over there.'

'Don't be bloody ridiculous.' He was cross. He'd always been short-tempered and the last few months had been a strain.

'I'm serious, sweetheart.' I moved to sit opposite him. 'I couldn't bear to go on without you.'

'You're insane, Beth. You're still a young woman. In perfect health.'

'Hardly young.'

'You're only sixty.'

'I mean it, Neil.' I put my hand over his. 'If you kill yourself, I'll throw myself under a train.'

'Then I can't do it, can I?' A muscle in his cheek twitched. 'I'll turn into a vegetable and make both our lives a misery. Is that what you want, you silly woman?'

'No,' I said. That wasn't what I wanted at all.

It started after Geoff's wife died. Madeline had been failing for years and, living next door, we'd seen the hell they went through in her final months. Her deterioration had been particularly depressing for Neil, who'd been reading articles about dementia sometimes being hereditary.

'It's like my Dad, all over again,' he'd said, with a shudder. 'If I ever get like that, I want you to finish me off. Take the carving knife to me. Promise?'

His father's house smelled. The bathroom, in particular, stank. It took a while for Neil to find out why. The poor old chap knew where he was supposed to go to urinate. But he'd forgotten what to do when he got there and simply peed all over the carpet. It was humiliating for everybody. When he finally died it was a relief.

'A meat cleaver might be more final,' I'd said, trying to lighten his mood. 'Though messier.'

It became a sick joke between us. Nothing serious. Then, over a few months, things changed dramatically. Neil had always mislaid keys and spectacles. I did myself, but he became incapable of finding anything. I put a china bowl on the kitchen dresser and suggested he use that as a collection point, but whenever he went there for something, it was empty.

'I'm losing the plot, aren't I?' he grumbled one day, after finally locating his house keys in the drawer where we kept the electrical leads. 'Why would I put them in there? My brain's turning to Swiss cheese.'

'All seventy-year-olds mislay things.' I gave him a hug. 'Tomorrow we'll buy you some vitamins. That might help.'

Several days later he accosted me in the greenhouse. He looked as if he didn't know whether to laugh or cry. 'Why were my spectacles in the fridge?'

'Whatever are you talking about?'

'My bloody spectacles were in our refrigerator. On top of the Flora.' He slapped the side of his head with his hand, as if to knock sense into it. 'I'm going bloody barmy, aren't I?'

'Sweetheart, we all do crazy things. Remember when I started to reverse the car out of the garage? With the up-and-over door still closed?'

'That's true.' He looked relieved, but not much.

However, days later, I looked out of the kitchen window and said: 'The bin, darling. It's Thursday. Didn't you put it out?'

Neil glanced up from *The Independent*. 'It's okay, I did it when I got back from the newsagents. Before I raked up those dead leaves at the bottom of the garden.'

'So where is it, then?'

He abandoned the paper and joined me at the window. 'Damned if I know. I expect the bin men emptied it and stuck it next door by mistake.'

They hadn't, of course. It was where it always was behind the shed. Still full.

'You *meant* to do it,' I said when he eventually came back inside. 'Sometimes I mean to clean the oven, but then conveniently forget. Probably because it's a chore.'

Neil paced up and down, like an animal in a trap. 'But it's not just the bin, Beth. Is it? I lost my electric razor yesterday, and my credit cards the day before. Then I left the bathroom tap running last night when I went to bed. I've no idea what I'm going to do next. It's a nightmare.'

'You're preoccupied, that's all. Though maybe you *should* see the doctor.'

'I'm damned if I want to be asked if I know what day of the week it is.'

'And what day is it?'

'It's Thursday. September the 25th.'

'There you are, my love. You're fine.'

The days dragged on until Geoff wandered in through the kitchen door one morning, as he often did, with some vegetables for us from his allotment.

'I could do with my mower back, if that's okay,' he said to Neil.

'Your mower?'

'You know, mechanical thingy that cuts grass and makes a godawful racket? That you borrowed from me at the weekend?'

Neil's fists clenched at his sides. 'I was planning to come over and ask you for it. Tomorrow.'

'But you've already got it, old man. That's why I need it back.' There was an awkward pause. 'Okay,' continued Geoff, looking embarrassed. 'Tell you what, you hang on to it and let me have it back when it's convenient.'

'But I don't have it,' Neil protested, looking at me. 'Do I?'

'It's in the garage,' I said, avoiding his eye.

There was a silence, before Geoff slapped Neil on the shoulder in a not-very-convincing show of bonhomie. 'Not to worry. I missed the dentist last month. He still charged me for the appointment, though. Grasping bastard.'

The incident hit Neil hard. 'I told you I was getting like Dad,' he said. 'This proves it.'

I wasn't sure what to say, so I kept silent. But I put my arms round his waist, buried my face in his scratchy sweater and gave him a hug.

'I'd rather be six foot under than lose my dignity,' he murmured into my hair, sounding close to tears.

'At least get a proper diagnosis,' I urged. 'What if you're wrong?'

'What's the point of a diagnosis? There's no cure, is there?' He extracted himself from my grasp and looked me in the eye. 'I've got to take matters into my own hands while I still can. I could deteriorate rapidly. The way Dad did. That's what scares me. Leaving it too late.'

'Don't do it, Neil. Please! I couldn't bear it.'

'You'll manage. People do. Look at old Geoff.'

'I refuse to talk about it.'

'But we must. Plans have to be made.' He took my hand in his and kissed it. 'I need you to understand,' he said. 'I would break my heart if you didn't.'

'I understand perfectly,' I said. 'I just don't agree.'

'Of course you don't. But you will support me?'

'You mean, hand you a full bottle of pills?'

'And get yourself in trouble with the law? No way. Assisted suicide's a crime. I wouldn't want to involve you in anything like that. And the Swiss clinic business raises too many legal questions. But I've done research on the internet. If I crash my car into that dirty great brick wall by the railway bridge, my worries will be over before I know what's happened. Especially if I choose a wet night, neglect to wear my seat belt and put my foot down. That way, the life insurance people shouldn't ask awkward questions.'

'Oh, Neil, don't talk like that. I've got my pension.'

'A fat lot of good that will do you. Just think of all the money we've shelled out over the years. They owe us.' He patted my arm. 'You deserve some happiness after I've gone. I refuse to leave you hard up.'

'Please, sweetheart,' I begged. 'Don't do this. I'll look after you, whatever happens. We promised, for better or worse.'

'Not another word, Beth. My mind's made up. We'll go away somewhere for a second honeymoon. Then come back and I'll do it.

When the time finally came, Neil and I kissed goodbye at the door before he went out to the car. We were both crying. Then I watched him drive off at speed into the night. Losing him like this would be hard, but he was right: life would go on.

I went back inside and picked up the phone to call Geoff. It had taken us three careful months of planning to get to this.

'Neil's just left, darling,' I said, when he answered. 'I've just got to wait for the traffic police to knock on my door. Then we're free.'

WOLFSBANE

by

Richard Hooton

It was the strangest interview he'd ever done. And there'd been plenty of weird ones. Jason smirked. But then his brow furrowed. *How do you know if someone's capable of killing?*

Questions prowled through his head. *Can you trust a stranger you want to hire for murder?* Most people are easy to read; their very appearance a betrayal. They were as obvious as a children's book. This guy said little. His eyes were like stones. He was a blank sheet; impossible to judge.

They sat at opposite ends of a stark wooden table. No tablecloth or place mats adorned it, just plates of food and cans of lager. Arms behind his head, Jason slouched back in his dining chair as he examined the man he knew as Thornton: short, black, slicked back hair, trimmed beard, smart suit, crisp shirt, plain tie; as if he'd come straight from the office. He was slim — Jason had expected someone muscular — with a narrow nose and thin lips.

He didn't look like a killer.

Unfurling his chubby hands from the back of his head, Jason grabbed his fork to shovel down curry. It left the roof of his mouth burning and his tongue numb. He washed it down with a swig of cold lager.

'Enjoying your food?' Thornton's tone was flat, devoid of feeling. He took a bite of his own meal, unflinching.

'It's alright.' Jason's nose streamed. 'No Gordon Ramsey though, are you?'

'I need my curry hot to warm me up. Terrible circulation. Too hot for you?'

'It's fine.' Jason plunged another forkful into his mouth to prove it. The room stank of garlic. But he was hungry.

'Hope you didn't mind me bringing it round to your place to heat up.' Thornton sniffed dryly. 'I'm particular about what I eat.'

Jason shrugged. 'Save's me making anything.'

'You can tell a lot about a man by how he eats.' Thornton chased a piece of meat around his plate with his fork. 'About his true nature.' The morsel slithered away. 'It's the same across the animal kingdom.' He stabbed the meat still with his fork before swallowing it whole.

Jason chewed on a piece of sinew. All this talk about food. He's so bland, unlike this curry.

He doesn't sound like a killer.

The contact seemed good. He was the man he was after, he'd said. He'd done it many times.

'How long you been married, Jason?' — 'Three years,' he replied, through a mouthful of brown gloop — 'Any kids?' He shook his head. 'That's a blessing.' Thornton carefully positioned his cutlery across his empty plate and wiped his mouth with a napkin.

He didn't act like a killer.

Jason saw he had plenty of food left himself and wolfed it down before clattering his fork onto his plate. He felt like jabbing Thornton with the fork just to provoke a reaction. A proper weapon was strapped to the underside of the table. He hoped he'd have no need to grab the gun.

'How will you do it?'

'I've a way that leaves no evidence. Nothing to trace us to the body.'

If something sounds too good to be true then ... Jason laughed. This guy wasn't convincing him. *He's not dangerous. Just odd. Another screwball.*

'So what's she done wrong?' asked Thornton. 'She a bad cook like me?'

Jason wiped sticky sweat from his brow with his shirt sleeve. 'You said the less you knew the better.'

'A divorce is less final.'

'There's a will – you're the way.'

Thornton didn't laugh. His green eyes flickered. Jason followed their gaze to the mantelpiece where a woman in a framed photograph smiled across at him. 'That her?' Jason nodded. She meant nothing to him. It was just a picture: flat, grey, two-dimensional. Should he mention an affair? Debts? *No real need.*

Thornton's eyes scanned the rest of the room, scrutinising the cheap furniture and simple decoration. 'Sure you can afford me?'

Jason scratched his stubble. He walked over to a sideboard, opening it up to pull out a large sports bag. He unzipped it to reveal wads of notes.

'Hundred grand, used notes, like we agreed.' He sat back down. 'Sure you're up to the job?'

Thornton leaned forward, his hands placed palm down. 'One guy hired me to get rid of his business partner. I set it up well with the rope. No policeman or pathologist would have suspected it wasn't suicide.' His voice was a hard monotone. 'Another wanted a road accident. That cost more, to take into account the vehicle I had to destroy afterwards. One guy really wanted his wife to suffer. Bit of torture with that one. Knives, electricity, blowtorch. He wanted her to know who'd ordered it.' He studied his filed fingernails. 'There are some sick, vicious people out there, Jason.'

Thornton attempted to smile. Despite the curry, Jason felt colder.

'The target always begs for their life. You should hear what they promise. They'll do anything to spare them, Jason. Absolutely anything. Never works.'

A thunderous bang erupted. Jason span round. It came from outside. He hesitated, fingers twitching.

Thornton didn't move. 'Sounded like a car backfiring. Don't panic.'

Jason scowled, running his nail-bitten fingers through his untidy mop of hair. He turned back to face Thornton. 'So what's your great plan?'

'Wolfsbane.'

'What?' *Was this guy for real?*

'It's a poisonous plant. Also called aconite, monkshood or the Devil's helmet. All interesting names but I prefer Wolfsbane. You know why it's called that, Jason?' He was suddenly animated. 'It means wolf killer. It was used to poison wolves. You know what's funny though?' Jason sighed. *Where's this going? I just need someone prepared to pull a trigger.* 'I read somewhere that it was also called Wifesbane. Wife killer. Perfect.' Thornton's tongue flickered over his lips. 'Its vivid purple flower has drooping petals, all hooded like a monk, hence the name. Such beautiful delicacy.' Jason looked again at the photograph: the dark hair draped over her shoulders, a dainty nose, red lips parted into an alluring smile, hooded eyes. 'You wouldn't believe it's capable of such venom.'

'Proper little horticulturist aren't you?'

'You might learn something. Maybe a bit of history? The ancient Greeks called it the "Queen of poisons." In Egypt, Cleopatra poisoned her brother with it. Your Queen will feel its sting.' Jason shifted in his chair. 'You've got to be careful though, it's so toxic it can soak through your skin and kill you. You need gloves. If I slip it in her drink, a few sips and she'll be dead.'

'If it's so deadly where'd you get it?'

'You just grow it. Someone I know has it in his garden. Best bit is it'll leave her bloodstream within hours. No one'll know what, or who, killed her.'

A loud knock at the front door, just yards away, silenced him. Thornton instinctively thrust his right hand into the inside pocket of his suit jacket. Jason reached under the table. His gun wasn't there.

'Expecting anyone?' hissed Thornton. 'Not come home early has she?'

'I don't know who it is. She's at her sister's.'

Jason stood up, then paused. The door rattled again, the knock sharp and insistent.

'I'll send them away,' he said.

'Don't answer it.' It was a command not a request. 'As far as anyone else is concerned there's no one in this house tonight.'

They sat in uncomfortable silence until certain they were alone. Thornton removed his hand from inside his suit. Jason sat back down. *Where the hell's my gun?* His hands were clammy and tingling. *It's the stress.* He tried taking deep breaths but found his breathing laboured. *Have I got enough?* He looked again into Thornton's eyes. Now, he saw confidence swirling with malevolence, encased in an icy cold blue. They revealed a truth the appearance tried to cover.

He's a born killer.

'Do you want me to kill her for you?' Menace threaded its way through the voice.

It was enough. Jason bobbed his head weakly. His stomach was in knots. He held his arm up to the light and stared at it. He felt the weirdest sensation, like hundreds of tiny ants were crawling over his skin.

'You alright, Jason?' There was no compassion in the question. Jason looked searchingly towards the front door. The room started to move, slowly at first as if on a boat on choppy waters, then spinning faster and faster like his chair had become a carousel. He touched his face but couldn't feel anything. The numbing sensation spread from his lips as if his nerve endings were being wiped away. His stomach burnt like the fires of hell were aflame inside him.

Jason turned to one side and a stream of sick spewed from his deadened lips, blackening the wooden floorboards. He gripped his chair, trying desperately to stay upright.

Thornton stood up, those fierce eyes burning with triumph. 'No one will hear you howl.'

Jason's limbs went numb. He lost his grip, collapsing to the floor, chair falling one way, his weakened body the other. His arms splayed across his own vomit. 'Please ... help me,' he whispered from his ravaged throat.

'You see.' Thornton gave a mirthless laugh. 'They always beg for mercy in the end.' He looked at his Rolex. 'The poison kills within six hours but the amount I gave you, you'll be dead in minutes. First you'll be paralysed, then blind, before your pitiful mind stops functioning.'

'You're ... a ... animal.' Jason laid still, puke dribbling down his chin.

'We're all animals, Jason. You're the wolf, savage and uncaring. The blood of reptiles flows beneath my skin.' Thornton carefully put his plate, cutlery and napkin in a carrier bag that held the containers he'd brought the food in and picked it up.

Jason looked at the photograph. 'She didn't ...'

'Your wife didn't get to me. I think for myself. The wolf is a predator that hunts weaker animals. My dilemma was this: Do I kill the wife or the wolf? Why kill the innocent wife when I can just kill the callous betrayer and no one would ever know?' He strolled to the sideboard from where he took the bag of money and hauled it over his shoulder. 'I'll just take my money leaving no trace I was ever here. The innocent doesn't die, the guilty is hoist with their own petard and I get my fee. What you're experiencing is the agonising pain your wife would have felt.' He smiled. 'If I hadn't spared her and taken your life instead.' Thornton strode towards the door. 'Your wife would have noticed the poison in her drink as well. Leaves a bitter taste, a burning sensation. I made your curry hot to cover it. Mine was milder.'

'…didn't … exist,' finished Jason.

Thornton froze. He glared at Jason and noticed a wire peeking out of his shirt. Footsteps clattered outside. Running. Getting louder.

'You're not who I thought you were,' he said coldly.

Jason groaned. 'You're who I wanted.' He crawled like a parched man in a desert towards the door, using all his strength to reach desperately for the handle.

Thornton pushed ahead of him. The door burst open. Three burly man barged in. Panic haunted their faces. 'Police. Freeze.' One shoved Thornton against the wall. 'You've tried to kill a detective,' he yelled, his expression a contortion of anger and distress.

'Too late,' said Thornton, calmly. 'He's a dead man.'

Distracted, the trio stared helplessly at their stricken colleague.

Unable to move, Jason looked at Thornton. This time, he saw the wide eyes of a wild animal — intense, unpredictable, base — stare back. *Interview over.* Just before his vision faded, he was the only one to see Thornton reach into his suit pocket and pull out his gun

THE PROMISE
by
M.D.Hall

Soon after the radio announcer cheerily communicated the possibility of black ice – for roads a hundred miles north of his position – Rob found his very own patch. *Typical*! he thought. After twenty minutes of trying to push his car out of the ditch, he gave up.

This was the last thing he needed on the night before Christmas. For each of the last two Christmas Eves he had not made it back home before the kids went to bed. His parting words to Jane, as he set off for work this morning, were: 'Don't worry, I'll be home on time. I've told my boss that come hell or high water I'm leaving early!' His wife had been right to look unconvinced, as once again he was about to let them down.

He opened the boot and looked at the 'surprise' presents. The shoes for Jane – he had noticed her snatching glances at them as they walked past Hargreaves' a couple of weeks ago. She wouldn't say anything, as she knew he was working every extra hour to pay for her mum's medical bills.

The heaviest parcel was Jack's new games console. It was the last thing Jack would expect – due to shipping problems, only a tiny number had made their way into the stores and Jack, like every other kid, would have to wait until after Christmas … Except,

Rob had a friend who knew someone, who knew someone else, who for a price could get one of the fabled boxes.

Adele – little Adele – never asked for anything, but lately she had been a little upset for Toby, her toy owl. He was lonely, and needed a friend. Actually, she was more specific ... he needed a girlfriend. Rob had no idea where to start looking for a 'girl' owl. He got around it, he hoped, by asking the shop assistant to tie a pink ribbon around *her* neck.

Now he had three parcels and a two mile walk to his house, nestled deep in the Northumbrian countryside. Jane had thought the move out of the city would be good for the kids. As a die-hard city dweller, Rob had his doubts; the area was certainly beautiful, but it was also remote. He made his views known, and soon they were ensconced in the home of Jane's dreams.

It was not long before they learned that the area was not quite the residential idyll they had imagined. Local rumours circulated about the locality being a retreat for less corporeal residents, while the nearby church had a congregation of precisely five, if Rob, Jane, the kids and the vicar were included. The nearest village was another three miles behind where his car had skidded off the road, and no one ever came this way.

Jack and Adele were very popular in the village school, but none of their classmates would visit; not that it bothered his kids – Adele was too young to notice, and she was invited to lots of parties, while Jack just thought that living in 'ghost central,' as he liked to call it, was cool.

None of them had ever seen a single ghost; not even a solitary odd occurrence that could not be explained. Tonight, however, the real horror of living here was brought home to Rob … walking two miles in leather-soled brogues on an icy road while carrying three parcels. Fortunately, the night sky was clear with a full moon, and there was no sleet or snow to hamper his walk.

He held his watch up to the boot's dim courtesy light, seven-thirty. He estimated forty-five minutes to cover the two miles, which meant, if everything went according to plan, he would be home by eight-thirty and in time to catch the kids before bedtime. He placed the games console under one arm. *Why do the boxes have to be so big?* he asked himself. Putting the string handles of the carrier bag containing the shoes into the hand of the same arm, he was ready for *operation boot close*. With the owl parcel close to the edge of the boot, he pressed the auto-close boot button before grabbing the parcel and pulling it out of the boot while there was still a large enough gap. He always felt a certain childish pride when he managed to do this on shopping trips, but was still at a loss to understand why car manufacturers did not properly equip the remote to close the boot.

It was not long before Rob realised his time estimate was way out. The road was even more treacherous than he had guessed, and it was only a matter of time before he fell and Jack's console became consigned to scrap. To make matters worse, a brisk wind had picked up and brought sleet lashing into his face, obscuring his sight.

His only hope of getting home on time was to cut through the wood. Here, at least, the ground would be broken and possibly not yet frozen – the presence of the trees might have kept the temperature above freezing. In any event, those same trees would break up the sleet.

He had no other option, yet still he hesitated. The wood that led towards his house also housed the church and graveyard, while the trees, normally so elegant, even in winter, took on the aspect of blackened skeletal hands reaching up from the earth. He stood at a mental crossroads. To stay on his current path would mean missing the kids' bedtime, and breaking yet another promise. How could he possibly consider risking the happiness of his children for a foolish, irrational fear? It was a no brainer, he couldn't.

Within a couple of minutes, he knew he had made the right choice. As hoped, the trees acted as a natural windbreak and the sleet turned to droplets of water. The ground was frozen, but only the surface, which allowed him to maintain his footing.

He had made good progress when what little wind there was, stilled. Even the dribble of defrosted sleet stopped, as though someone had tightened a dripping tap. What struck him even more was the absolute, the utter silence that pervaded the entire wood. Rob stopped, and listened – he had never before experienced a complete absence of sound. He scrubbed his foot against an exposed root, but even that produced no sound.

The moon bathed the soundless wood in a cold, stark light, lending an even more cadaverous aspect to the wizened trees. Then from the corner of his eye, he caught a glimpse of something dark. He turned, but saw nothing. Yet as he looked towards that spot – beyond which lay the graveyard – he was filled with a hollow dread.

At that very moment, not a hundred yards away, something materialised in his line of sight. He had no name for it – the best description he could muster was *smudge*. It was roughly the height of a man, but it was impossible to make out the shape … shapes. For as he stood transfixed, other *smudges* appeared to the sides and behind the original. Each shape was stock-still.

The dread became a loathing. He needed to escape, but how could he outrun things that could appear at will? Sweeping aside the impossibility of his situation, he propelled his reluctant legs as fast as they would carry him; more than once stopping to pick up a fallen parcel. Now the *smudges* were moving, some positioning themselves to cut him off, while the others steadily advanced upon him. The forced realisation that the parcels were slowing his progress broke his heart, but he had no other option. Dropping them, he continued running through the cold, bright, silent nightmare.

All at once, he broke through the edge of the wood; his house only two hundred yards across a fallow field. He did not turn to see what was behind him, but was aware that the *smudges* seeking to cut him off had faltered. *Is it the lights of the house making them wary?* he wondered, daring to hope that the life-force within his home was giving the creatures pause for thought. Whatever their reasons, he felt renewed hope surge through his being.

The field soon behind him, he vaulted the short stone wall bordering his house and ran across the lawn, fumbling in his pocket for his house keys ... and found them.

Almost stumbling as he rushed pell-mell towards the front door, he slotted the key into the lock and turned the barrel. The door did not open – it seemed almost welded shut.

Leaving the keys dangling in the lock, he ran to the lounge window and looked inside. Jane sat on the settee, her arms around Jack and Adele, both dozing as she looked fondly from one to the other. To the side was the tree, festooned with ornaments and lights, with presents arrayed beneath. The room was bathed in a golden glow from a couple of wall lights, but mostly from the welcoming fire in the hearth. Rob's heart soared; Jane had kept the kids up beyond their bedtime, waiting for their dad.

He raised a hand to bang on the window, and felt a grip on his shoulder. A cold he had never known swept through his body as he felt an irresistible compulsion to turn around. With all his strength, he fought to avert his eyes from what was behind him, but to no avail.

What stared back at Rob had once been human, but not for a long time. Clothed in rags, the creature's limbs were visible in part through the rent fabric, flesh curling away from sinew and rotted muscle. Despite his revulsion it astounded him how such a *thing* could muster any strength at all. His out of place reverie was interrupted by a croaking voice – he could see the vibrating, lacerated windpipe. 'This Christmas is not for you!'

'Get back you … Get back!' He tried to pull away from the inhuman grip, but instead of breaking free, found himself compelled towards the small car parked on the drive – Jane's car. The creature forced him down until he was looking into the side window. What he saw caused him to gag. His reflection was missing the topmost part of the skull, and the neck was at such an angle it was clearly broken. Then he remembered spinning-off the road and smashing into a tree. When was that? Last year? Two years ago? He thought of the scene on the settee – Jack and Adele seemed a little older than when he left home.

The restraining hand was removed, and Rob stood up. He looked at the field, at the now definite forms as they stood expectantly. His gaze swept past the familiar figures and was drawn to the pointed spire of the church set back within the wood, standing proud of the bare, black trees … a beacon.

He glanced back at the house – his cold, dead heart swelling with an unutterable sadness – and wondered how many times he had tried to keep his promise, and how many more times he would try.

The croaking voice spoke again, 'This is no place for us. It is no place for you. Come home.'

21630612R00157

Printed in Great Britain
by Amazon